RATTLED

A DEVIL'S HANDMAIDENS MC NOVEL

ALASKA CHAPTER
BOOK 2

E.M. SHUE

Rattled

DEVIL'S HANDMAIDENS MC
Alaska Chapter Book 2

AWARD-WINNING AUTHOR
F.M. SHUE

Award-Winning Author

E.M. SHUE

DEVIL'S HANDMAIDENS MC ALASKA

Text Copyright ©2024 E.M. Shue

All rights reserved. This book or parts thereof may not be reproduced in any form, stored in any retrieval system, or transmitted in any form by any means—electronic, mechanical, photocopy, recording, or otherwise—without prior written permission of the publisher, except as provided by United States of America copyright law. For permission requests, write to the publisher, at "Attention: Permissions Coordinator," at the address below.

This is a work of fiction. Names, characters, places, and incidents either are the products of the author's imagination or are used fictitiously. Any resemblance to actual persons, living or dead, businesses, companies, events, or locales is entirely coincidental.

Cover Design by Mountain Rose Press

Formatting by Mountain Rose Press

Editing by Nadine Winningham of The Editing Maven

www.authoremshue.com

emshue.ak@gmail.com

❦ Created with Vellum

TRIGGER WARNING

Rattled contains hot and steamy sex, profanity, drinking, breath play, drugs, kidnapping and sex trafficking, on page attempted rape, off page rape, off and on page physical abuse, teenage pregnancy, graphic violence, murder and may contain other content that could be sensitive to some readers. Rattled is meant for mature reading audiences, 18+.

RATTLED

River "Jinx" Schmidt has closed off her heart after Reaper's betrayal. Returning to her hometown with her best friend and MC club hasn't been the welcoming distraction she'd hoped for. The town holds too many painful memories of the parents she lost when she was a teen. Every day, she slides further and further into depression and her art, seeking solace in her own world when she can.

Klay "Reaper" Ulrich regrets hurting Jinx and abandoning her the way he did. After turning his back on his career, he chases after the woman he loves. Reaper reenters her life without warning, determined to win her back. He'll make her understand he had no other option. Both their lives depended on the choice he made the fateful day he lost her.

Then an enemy from Reaper's past surfaces in Alaska. All of the secrets and lies Reaper has told come back to haunt him. When Jinx is taken, Reaper will kill to get her back. But with time running out and Jinx left in the Wilds of Alaska, she'll have to learn it's not just physical strength but heart that she needs to save herself.

Join Surprises from E.M. to be kept up to date.
 https://bit.ly/SurprisesfromEM

For those that dream and believe in luck.

ONE
REAPER

I pull up to the large warehouse and wait for the gate to open, then I input the code on my phone for the large bay door. My motorcycle rumbles between my legs, and I feel the grit covering my body. It vibrates off me in a cloud, like Pigpen from Charlie Brown. All I do is work. I barely eat or sleep.

I've been pushing through to finish this case and close out what I can. I've arrested many of the men in the group, but I'm missing the money man—the leader and gunrunner. I'm sure I know who it is, but my superior keeps telling me it can't be him. The new pain-in-my-ass bureaucrat who now oversees my unit says the guy is dead and gone. But my gut keeps telling me he's out there. The death rumors are just that. Rumors. I need to get this all taken care of before I walk away from everything I've known and become whatever life has in store for me next. I don't care as long as I'm with her. It's been like this for months now. I'm bone-tired and everything aches. The worst is my heart, and I can't make the pain stop. The ache in my heart is now dull compared to what it was eight months ago when one text message changed everything in my life.

That text was an image of an arrest warrant for the woman I love. She was going to be arrested in connection with the disappearance of a man who was a known human trafficker and for interfering in legal proceedings. The charge wasn't farfetched. My background check had shown that the missing man had a connection with another Devil's Handmaiden. The DHMC is the group my girl rides with. My baby girl helped rescue her fellow MC member from him. Word is that the DHMC helps fight human trafficking, and the rider they saved was underage when they rescued her. She's now become a part of the DHMC too. It was very possible my girl had something to do with it, but I wasn't going to risk her life because some bureaucrat thought he could advance his career and force me to do what he wanted. The latter charge was trumped-up. All she did was answer my secure ATF phone. My new division chief has it out for me and my woman. I've done a lot to protect her. I've even made sure she's taken care of in the event something happens to me. I'm not above bribery and coercion to protect the woman I love.

I thought all I'd have to do was walk away for a short time and close the fucking case. But this case is never-ending case. No matter what I do, I'm thwarted at every turn. I'm fairly certain the bureaucrat who fucked up my life is on the take and preventing me from closing it. It has to be Division Chief Drawer because my handler, Anderson, has been with me since I first started. We didn't have issues until this case and since Drawer came in. As for the gunrunner who Drawer insists is dead, Lucifer was a case I almost closed five years ago, but he somehow found out and disappeared and went underground. From some research I've been doing, I've found that's when Drawer started working his way up the chain of command at ATF. He has links to several politicians in DC. He came over from Homeland Security and is now a division chief. I need to get someone to do a deeper dive into him. I know who, but I'm so pissed at him right now. If I see him, I'd strangle him for what he's done to hurt my woman. Regardless of our relationship.

I think about the first moment I saw River "Jinx" Schmidt and decided that my career could be fucked. I wanted her and I was going to have her. It didn't matter that I was close to closing my biggest case. When the moment came, I tied her to me, and my only regret is walking away. Then one month ago everything changed when my sweet River moved away from Kentucky and back to her home in Alaska. I can't watch over her and make sure she's safe. I can't watch her from afar. I can't see her anymore. What if another man has started sniffing after her? What if she is able to get the divorce she's been trying to get from me?

I park my bike and know I'm not alone. I have an unwelcome guest. One, my dog, who I moved here instead of leaving at my place in Widow's Creek, isn't rushing down to meet me. And two, I see Titan's bike sitting there. I sit on my bike for a moment longer as I try to control my anger. The fury doesn't dissipate. It burns so bright in my chest. Because of him, getting River back is going to be much harder. He fucked me over, and I'm ready to knock out his teeth. Our relationship be damned.

I swing off my bike and slip my helmet over my handlebars. I proceed to the stairs and take them two at a time up to my apartment. Fueled by rage, I push the door open hard enough to impale into the wall. Trigger runs for me but stops and backs off, knowing I'm not in the mood to say hello. I keep moving and don't stop until I'm in Titan's face.

"You are a fucking idiot. You hurt my wife. Now, it's going to be harder for me to fix our issues." I pull back my arm and slam my fist into his face hard. His nose instantly crumples from the impact. He's a couple of inches shorter than me but has a bit more bulk. "Why?" I grab his T-shirt under his cut and slam my fist into his face again, hitting him in the jaw this time. I guide his ass to the barstool so he doesn't fall over, thus protecting him from getting hurt further. That's what brothers do.

"Fucker. I was helping you." He rubs his jaw as he

works it, opening and closing it over and over. He reaches up and wipes the blood from his nose. "You fucking broke my nose again."

I'm beyond angry. He set me up to look bad in front of Ginger, one of River's friends. I dive for him, and we slam into the bar. Bottles rattle and fall, shattering on the floor around us.

"Fuck, little brother, stop it," he barks as he hits me back. It's what I want and need. I fall back and feel blood drip down my chin. "Are you happy?" He holds up his fists, ready to hit me again.

"No, I'm not happy." I huff as I wiggle my fingers at him in a come get me gesture. "I want out. I need out. I have to go to her." I move toward him, swinging again. He dodges and hits me in the ribs. I take the hit and roll with it, slugging him in the side of the head. His next words stop me.

"Yes, you do." He stands back with his hands up, waiting to see what I'll do next. When I don't move, he turns to pour us each a couple fingers of whiskey. I take the offered glass and throw it back in one shot. The burn of the alcohol and the pain of the hit don't dull the ache in my heart.

"Why?" I growl and clench my teeth.

"Because she's in danger. Phantom is out and dropped off the map. I've been searching for him, but he's got someone helping him." He points at his laptops over on the table. I see them both open and running software. I move over and see that he's running facial recognition on Phantom. Phantom is a man who attacked my woman and her best friend, Scout. I already killed his brother to protect River, and I'll kill him next if I have to.

"They won't let me out."

"You already quit. Your retirement papers and resignation letter will be sent Monday." He shrugs as he comes to stand next to me. He's shoving napkins up his nose to stop the bleeding.

"Come here." I walk over to the kitchen sink and turn on the water. Grabbing a dishcloth out of the drawer, I run it under the cold tap. He steps up to me, and I wipe his face and grip his nose tight as I move my hand, setting the bone. We learned to do this to each other years ago. When we were separated in foster care, we still fought with everyone else around us. Titan is almost four years older than me. He aged out of the system before I did, but he was always watching me.

He's the one I contacted after I got the text and had to walk away from River. He was able to get a unit into Snake's house to get the women out of there who were being trafficked and pimped out. Titan made sure the women were cared for and sent back to their homes. River had wanted to get them out and struggled with the fact that we had to leave them at Snake's plantation. That's why I got Titan involved.

"Thanks, brother." He thumps my shoulder. "I can't go with you because I need to run those checks you wanted me to do on Anderson and Drawer. I've also been running a check on Lucifer." He pauses, and

I know what he's going to say. I start to protest, but he holds his hand up. "No, listen. There is nothing. If he's out there, he's changed his appearance drastically and has been lying low, but I agree that it was too convenient."

"Thanks. How long until I can leave?"

"Two weeks. I'm pretty sure Phantom is already up there causing issues, but he knows to keep his face covered."

"How did he get out?"

"He flipped." Titan huffs and runs his hand through his long hair. He pulls it back, and I watch as he takes the tie from his wrist to put it into a man bun. "You better get a haircut and trim before you take off." He laughs as he points at me. Trigger walks over and leans his big body into my leg.

"I will." I give Trigger a pat on his head then look up at Titan. He's staring at me like he knows what I'm about to ask. "Is she okay?"

His lips tip up slightly. "She started racing again, but she misses you. She's been struggling."

He walks over to his laptops and opens another window on one of them. After a few clicks, he turns it toward me, and I watch a video feed of my girl. She's in her painting gear in the main part of an auto shop. I watch her walk over to a door and press her ungloved finger to a pad then pull it open.

"I need to log off," Titan says as he slips between me and the laptop. He closes the window and then clicks on several other screens. "Whoever is running their security is good. I have to change my VPN regularly and can't be on their cameras too long."

Titan taps away on his laptop, then another video screen pops up. This feed is from the outside of the auto shop. I see two other businesses in front of it.

"Where is that?" I ask.

"Ptarmigan Falls. There's the shop and restoration business, a saloon, a diner, and then the clubhouse." He points out each building.

"Who runs it all?"

"They do." His words don't really shock me because I ran backgrounds on all of the women mine associates with. Also, I needed to know as much as I could about Scout when my investigation started, before I fell for River.

"Is there a place I'll be able to stay close by? My woman is going to take some convincing before I can stay with her." I thump him hard on the back.

"Yeah, in Fairbanks. I think the Maiden's clubhouse used to be a small hotel, but it's been converted. Did you know Riddler's father owned all that? Or that he was one of the founders?"

"No. Anything on his murder?"

"No. Also, just so you know, Riddler was attacked recently."

He pulls up the hospital report detailing what Scout went through. I don't bother asking how he got access to her medical records because he wouldn't tell me.

"Did you know Riddler's got a relationship with an Alaska State Trooper?" Titan raises an eyebrow.

I chuckle at the irony that River is with me, an ATF agent, and her best friend, Scout—or Riddler, as she goes by her road name—is with a policeman. "Figures."

"I'll get background on him for you before you take off."

"How long are you going to be here? Does Prez know you're here?"

Only our president with Drago Defiance MC knows that we are biological brothers. We don't tell anyone. Not even ATF knows. Titan goes by his road name and not his birth name. His work is so top secret that not many know he even exists. He also cleared both of our records so no one can dig up our past. He's so good at his job that even the agency he works for is afraid of what he can do.

"You need to come with me," I beg him. I feel like if I leave him here things could happen. When I was in the military, it was hard for us to be apart. We both worried about each other. Being raised the way we were with drug addicted parents, we've always been protective of each other.

"I can't. I have to keep our covers here. I need to make sure you aren't followed."

"A, please." I call him the nickname I gave him years ago before he changed to his road name. We always used our initials growing up because we were teased over our names. They were so different from the other kids' names. Except now, I love when River calls me Klay. I love the breathy sound of her voice when she says it while I'm making love to her. I need to get her back. It's the only thought I have. My purpose in life.

"No, K. I have to do this. I'll keep in contact."

He packs up his laptops and then walks out. I sit down and look at the picture on my phone that I took of River the last time I saw her. She's curled up against my pillow with her naked back facing the camera. Her long curly hair is in disarray around her. I'd fucked her hard earlier that night. All of her sexy tattoos that line her back and body are on display for my eyes. I can't wait until the day she'll let me mark her skin with my machine. I flip to the next picture of her. It's my favorite. Her, in the pure-white gown, the night I made her mine. Till death do us part.

TWO
RIVER

I stand under the shower spray and let the water slide down my body. I look down and watch as the paint I got all over me runs down the drain. I took the day off from the shop and painted at the house today. I needed a release. The pain of everything is building up.

I knew coming back here was going to hurt, but I never expected it to hurt this much. It probably doesn't help that their house is still mine. It was supposed to be sold along with my father's car, but Scout's dad, Levi, had bought both of them thinking I would want them someday. He was kind of right. I do miss them, and having these things brings them back to me, but the pain is almost too much at times.

There are some days I'm glad I have more of them than the wedding rings I wear on a necklace every day. My parents' clothes aren't there, but pictures, knickknacks they collected from their travels, and my father's military memorabilia are on display throughout the house. The house is similar in design to the shop that Scout, my best friend, owns and I work out of. The main floor is a huge garage with a large three-bedroom house sitting above. I don't go upstairs very often, but I currently have the garage full of all my artwork. I've been painting like crazy since last October. Since he left me broken more than I was when my parents died.

After Klay married me and then left me, I purged all the pain from our breakup into my artwork. I finished reading the diary I got in Pandora regarding the brooch I found. I've used it for inspiration in all of my latest work. The brooch is the main focal point as well as the Druid priestess in most of the pieces. What Vixen saw before was minor compared to what I have now.

It was a shock to find my father's car here in what is now Scout's shop. The car I had wanted sold because the pain was too much. It was the first vehicle I ever painted and holds so many more memories of working with my father on it. I'm glad Levi didn't sell it like I'd requested, but it still hurts to see it. I haven't driven it at all. It's been in the garage since I moved back here in May. Scout keeps asking me if she can pull it out and check the engine.

My heart aches every day for Klay. I still don't know why he left me alone, but one day I'll find out, and I'll make him pay for the pain he's caused me. I gave him my heart and he lied to me. I only asked that he never leave me. But the first chance he got, he walked away from me. He didn't do it while I watched either. No, he left me while I was sleeping.

I don't go to many club parties usually, but our president and my best friend, Riddler, wants me to be there for this one. It's our first casual major club interaction with other MC clubs. I go to her saloon that's adjacent to our shop and the clubhouse, but I don't hook up with men. I act like I'm having fun and moving on, but I can't. Klay, Reaper, is the only man who has ever made me feel the way he did. He knew what I needed in bed and out. He told me he'd protect me and always be there for me, but he's gone now, proving that everyone leaves me. That I'm destined to be alone.

I've tried to understand this when I look at Scout and Thad, her ex. Thad is trying to make amends for the hurt and destruction of the past, but Scout has a hard time moving on. She looks at the fact that we belong to a motorcycle club and he's an Alaska State Trooper. We aren't like the one percenter clubs, but we don't always walk the line of the law. I've done some things in the past to protect others that I don't regret, but others would say it's wrong. To me, what is wrong is the legal system allowing men who prey on innocent women to get away with it. How the criminals use the judicial system to put the victims on trial instead of themselves. Maybe that's why I still protect Klay's secrets. Why I didn't even tell Scout, who knows just about everything about me, that Klay is with ATF or that we got married. Because I know that what he does, he does to help others.

The water hasn't started running cold yet, but I need to hurry. I grab the bottle of my rose-scented shampoo and wash out my long wavy hair. As I move my hands over my body, I think of the weight I've lost. I eat enough just to sustain my body. I don't crave anything but him anymore, and I'll never have him again.

Last month I got to run a drag bike, which is something I would have loved in the past. The adrenaline rush would have been more than an orgasm for me then, but it didn't have the same feeling as it did before. That's how I met Klay. His club, Drago Defiance, had wanted me to race their bike. But an investor wanted to meet me first, and that's when Klay said he fell for me. The first time he saw me in that bar. The investor was named Snake. He wanted to sleep with me. Klay stepped in and proclaimed I was his in order to protect me. Snake called his bluff and forced us to marry to prove we were a real couple, or he'd give me to Crazy, another biker, who was an enemy of mine. I had helped put his brother, Phantom, in prison. Crazy had threatened both Scout and me in court that he would kill us.

I finish my shower and move into my room. I have

a room in Scout's house, but I've moved into the clubhouse now that her mom is staying with her. Her mother's house was burned and vandalized. So she's been staying with Scout for protection. I don't want to be in the way, and it's a little too much for me to be around all of them at times. I don't want Scout to know how depressed I've gotten.

I wake up every day for Scout and her daughter, Skyler, but now that Thad is in their life it makes me wonder if I'm useless now. Maybe they don't need me anymore. But maybe it's time to find another reason to live. I thought it was Klay, but now I don't know. I don't know if I'm strong enough to live for just myself.

I get dressed in a pair of blue jeans that are tight, low rise, and shredded up and down the front. I pair them with a black leather corset halter top with silver grommets. The corset pushes my full breasts up, putting them on display. I style my hair straight, pulling the curls and waves out of it. My makeup is dark around my eyes, and my lips are a deep red. After I slip on a pair of high-heeled boots, I grab a thin leather jacket and slip my cut over it and then move out of my room. I make sure the door is locked when I close it.

"Dang, Jinx, ready to party tonight?" Ginger calls me by my road name as she walks over and squats down a bit to hip check me. I laugh and smile at her. She's almost six feet tall on her own. "You ready to move on, because there is a guy over there asking for you?" I follow her head tilt and look over to see one of the local coalition riders is checking me out. When his eyes move over my body, I try to hide the cringe of revulsion.

"I met him last month at the races," I clarify and nod at him as I move out the door. As the vice president of the club, I have to check on my president.

I walk over to the shop to see if Scout needs anything before the party starts.

Klay

I arrived in Fairbanks last night, and today I'm getting everything arranged to head out and check on my girl. I have to get Trigger set up in the new yard. He's running around the fence line sniffing everything. Everything is new. Every smell. Every tree and grassy spot. I hide my chuckle over him acting like a puppy.

I've rented a property north of the town of Fairbanks, just off Chena Hot Springs Road, but not in Ptarmigan Falls. I'm hoping I can get River under control and make my amends with her fairly quickly. I want to get us moved into a house permanently out there. I've already been looking for property and places to buy.

I know it's going to take some time. She isn't going to forgive me easily because of what Titan did and because I really hurt her when I walked away. I had told her repeatedly that I would protect her, but all she wanted from me was to be there. I know she struggles with abandonment issues because of her parent's deaths. She feels guilty too because it was her idea to have them come home early.

Those are things I'm going to have to focus on. I need to reassure her that I won't leave her again. That I only left to protect her, which has always been my main focus. I look at my cell and see the message from Titan with the latest information. I need to get to her because I'm sure trouble is on its way or already here for her.

"Trigger," I holler my big bloodhound's name. He lopes over to me, and I rub his head. His ears flop around along with all his folds. "Watch the house. Be a good boy." I step back inside the house and make sure the extra-large dog door is unlocked so he can get in and out. I don't know how long I'll be gone, but I've left him food, water, and I have eyes on the place as well.

I head out and move to my bike. I left my truck back in Kentucky with Titan at the warehouse. I drove my Escalade up here with my bike in the trailer, along with a couple more and some things I didn't want to leave behind.

I swing my leg over the bike and settle down into the seat. I have the longer seat on it so my baby girl will be able to ride with me. I've dreamed of her wrapped around my body as we ride. I turn out of the driveway and head toward Steese Highway. I look back into the valley below me and see the city of Fairbanks behind me.

When I get into Fox five minutes later, I notice an Alaska State Trooper SUV in front of me. I follow it up past the area the locals call Hilltop and then down into the valley of Ptarmigan Falls. I can see why my girl loved this country, but I can also bet that because of how small everything is and remote there are a lot of memories for her.

I pull over in the gas station and watch as the trooper vehicle pulls through the fence into the yard where my girl is supposed to be. I grab my cell phone that has another alert on it. Titan messaged that he is searching for footage of Phantom crossing the border into Alaska. But he's found some information that could get us in the clear with Drawer, the division chief who has been jonesing for me. I'm hoping we can get him taken care of soon so I don't have to tell River the real reason I walked away from her. I know she'll be mad at me when she finds out. More so than she already is.

Drawer fought my retirement and stated he was going to press charges if I walked away. I went to a higher-up, breaking the chain of command, in order to get permission to leave. But now Titan says that he's found some wire transfers from a bank in the Cayman Islands to Drawer. He'll get the proof, and we'll find out who is yanking his chain. He's also cleared Anderson, which was important to me. Anderson was my handler for years. I couldn't have the man I trusted so much be bad. He literally held my life in his hands when I was undercover.

THREE
RIVER

I stand by my president's side, taking in Thad and his friend, Dylan, who is also a trooper. They're here in an official capacity. I hate that Scout is going through this after her father was murdered. It's why we came home to Alaska sooner than anticipated. Scout had always planned to return someday, and of course I'd follow. After her dad was killed, she couldn't leave her mom here alone, thus moving up the timeline. When Brazen, our club president in Kentucky, made Scout the president of this chapter, I wasn't surprised. I was, however, shocked when Scout looked at me and made me her vice president. This is my family and will always be. Watching both Badger and Scout have to relive what their loved ones went through when they died is almost too much. It brings back memories of my own that I've struggled to control for the last two months. Every breath from my lungs aches as I remember the night the Alaska State Troopers along with Scout's dad came to tell me my parents died.

It looks like whoever killed Scout's dad also killed Badger's sister, who had been missing for months. I'm about to reach for Scout when my world shifts. The foundation of everything I've believed rattles into dust.

"I asked you before if you had any enemies. We have not been able to confirm if Mr. Smith is still being detained."

Both of us stop breathing. I've battled Crazy, and he met a bullet. Klay put him down because he was going to kill me. But Phantom, his brother, is still alive and in prison for almost killing Scout and attacking me. He has to be.

"He isn't," a voice I never thought I'd hear again says.

I don't realize I gasp, but I'm in motion. I can't stop my body, and for only a brief moment, I think of jumping into his arms. But that's it, one moment. I want to hurt him like he did me.

"Reaper?"

Klay is here, standing in front of me. I rear back and swing. My hand connects with his face in a loud crack that causes others to gasp. I'm normally level-headed and calm, but I'm not right now. All I want to do is make him feel some of the pain he's made me feel for the last nine months.

"What the fuck are you doing here?" I rail at him. I want to punch and kick him. Rage bubbles through my veins. My palm burns, but I don't care.

Klay rubs his cheek and chuckles. "Guess I deserved that."

That deep chuckle causes tingles to erupt across my skin. I remember him chuckling against my body, and I shake my head to stop the memories. I need the hate, or I will fall apart from the loss.

"You fucking think. You left me. You fucking left me in that room." The tears are right there, wanting to come out. Demanding to be let out, but I don't cry for him anymore. I can't. I did that enough. I cried for weeks until they dried up and I was left a shell of who I used to be.

"Baby," he says, and moves to pull me into his body, but I'm aiming to hit him again. He stops me and holds me to him. "We have a lot to talk about. I came for you. I had to take care of business, and then I came for you." He looks down at me, and I look up into his eyes. I see the emotion in them that only he lets me see, but the pain is too much.

"Well, go to hell. I don't want you." I yank away from his grip and go stand with Scout. The place I belong is next to my president.

Scout's giving him the death glare. She helped pick me up after he broke me. She was there when I first came home from Pandora and then later when Ginger saw him with another woman.

"Officers…" Klay looks at Thad and Dylan. "Troopers, sorry. You'll find out that one Stanley "Phantom" Smith is no longer in the state of Kentucky custody. He was paroled several months ago."

"How do you know that?" Thad barks at him.

I know this angers Thad because he just wants to protect Scout and Skyler, but he can't if he doesn't have all the information. Thad also doesn't know what Klay's real job is. No one but me does.

Klay looks past them to where I'm standing with most of the Devil's Handmaidens. "I can't tell you that." He doesn't know what I've told them about us. He doesn't know that I've kept his and our secrets. But he needs to tell us if Phantom is free. Phantom would be after both Scout and me and a few of the sisters too.

"Yes, you fucking can. If Phantom is coming after Riddler, we need to know." I grind my teeth as I move back toward him. I'm drawn to him still. Maybe I can fuck him and get him out of my system. But deep down I know I can't do that. I can't go there because he's not a one and done for me. He was supposed to be my forever.

"Baby, let me talk to these guys alone. You go inside and get me a beer."

I hit him again with a closed fist this time. Fucker is trying to order me around like I'm his old lady. He lost that chance when he snuck out on me. Left me in that bed naked and satiated from his fucking.

"Yep, deserved that too." He holds his jaw as he looks down at me. "Keep it up, baby girl, and I'm going to fuck you against that wall to prove who owns you," he says loud enough that everyone standing around hears him. I want to hit him again.

"Try it and I'll stick you with your Bowie," I bite out as I raise my brow at him.

"Reaper, what are you doing here?" Scout interrupts us.

"Can we talk?" He works his jaw. I feel a little bad but not enough to apologize to him. "Damn, baby, your hit has gotten better." He chuckles until he looks over at me. I'm clenching and flexing my fingers that hurt from hitting him. I know he's got a tough jaw, but I couldn't stop myself. This man drives me crazy, and not in a good way. Before I know it, he's in front of me again. "Fucking A, baby girl." He takes my hand in his big, tattooed ones as he pulls me into him. I can't stop myself from leaning in. I hate to admit it, but I've missed him. I take a deep breath, getting his scent in me, and it's like a hit of drugs to my system. "You can't damage your fingers, you know that. I'm sorry." He leans down and brushes his lips against my forehead. I try to fight him, but I'm not as strong as him. Plus, as his scent washes over me, I'm lost to all the memories. "You can come too." He drags me along with them. I'm at a loss here.

"Let's go to my office," Scout says as we start moving through the clubhouse with the troopers following behind us.

We are prepping for a party in celebration of Golden Days. I look over and see the guy from earlier checking me out again. Klay must notice him watching me because I hear a slight growl he tries to cover. I still affect him too. I almost want to cheer on the inside, but then I think of the fact he had another woman's ass on his dick. I start to struggle, but he holds fast, his grip tightening around my waist.

As soon as we step into Scout's office, Klay takes a chair and pulls me down onto his lap. I try fighting him again, but his arms band tight around me. This was how he held that woman. A wave of nausea washes over me, and I think of him fucking her like he did me. Of him giving her orders too. Of him choking her. His big, tattooed hand wrapped around her neck. I almost gag, but I hold it back and focus on the situation at hand.

Thad stands there looking like he wants to go to Scout, but he remains where he is and pulls off his wide-brimmed trooper hat before he looks at Klay and me.

"River, do I need to help you?" he offers.

I've known Thad a long time. He has been protective of me too, in a big brother way. I'm about to respond when Klay interrupts my thoughts.

"Dude, I don't know you, but you don't want to come between—" I cover his mouth, afraid of what he's going to say. What if he tells them we are married? Because we still are married. I haven't been able to file the divorce papers. It's like he knows I haven't told anyone. When he looks me in the eye, slowly raising that tattooed eyebrow, I can't stop the shiver. He sees it and knows what he does to me. That he still affects me.

"I was asking River," Thad says, breaking our connection. I'm glad because I almost leaned in and kissed him.

Klay starts to move me off his lap to go at Thad, but I hold him down. I don't want him fighting, and I can't let any of my secrets come out. I need to get him away from here. I decide I'll get him focused on me by challenging him. I'm still shocked he's here in Alaska. I need to find out the real reason why. He could have called and told us Phantom might be here. He didn't need to come. He doesn't need to lie that he's here to get me. I won't fall for his deceptions again.

"Thad, it's okay. I know how to handle Reaper myself." I smile down at Klay as I shift in his lap and mouth "Master." His eyes flare wide. Oh yeah, I got him now.

"Okay, Reaper, what do you want to talk to us about? Why wasn't I notified? I should've been," Scout says before I can get him distracted enough to take me out of the room and prove he's my Master. Damn it.

Klay pulls my hand away from his mouth and kisses my palm. I'm fucked now because I didn't tell Scout everything. She's going to find out who he really is. I grit my teeth and pinch my lips. I'm so pissed off with him. He stands up and answers her question.

"You should've been notified, but I don't think the authorities want to let you know they lost him a week after he went on parole. He up and disappeared. If you are having issues, I know it's him." My body locks up. If Phantom is here, Scout is in a lot of danger. He could have been behind all of this. The attack on her. The murder of her father. All of it fits his personality.

"He was supposed to serve a minimum of ten years, even if he got good behavior, because of the aggression of his attack. He also attacked the officers who arrested him." Scout stands and starts pacing. Thad moves to hold her to his body.

"Well. Well. Well. Riddler found herself a man. It's about fucking time." Klay chuckles, and I want to smack him again for her. She turns to glare at him. If looks could kill, he'd be a shriveled up shell of the man he is now.

"Continue. How do you know he's out? How do you know all this?" Thad is getting irritated with Klay. He is the one I'm going to have to be careful around because something about him causes Klay to become more aggressive. But thankfully now that Klay knows Thad and Scout are together, he won't be jealous and start spouting the truth about our relationship.

Klay takes a deep breath and looks at me before he turns back to Scout and Thad. I want to slam my hand over his mouth and stop the words that are going to come out. "I'm former ATF. I was under for the last eight years. I can't show you a badge or anything, but..." He reaches into his pocket and pulls out his wallet. He opens it and pulls out a card. "He'll be able to verify who I am. My real name is Klay Ulrich." He sits back down and pulls me back into his lap. His gaze is focused on me as he looks me in the eye, his hand holding my chin. "I'm here to get my woman back, to protect her from Phantom, and to warn you." I see the truth in his eyes, but I can't let him go there. He turns to Scout and nods before he turns back to me. "In that order, babe. I quit. Walked away because I'm not going to keep putting either of us in danger." My heart hurts, and my breathing is shallow as I take in the look in his eyes and the words he's saying. I can't let him back in, but I want to so badly. Every part of my heart wants to believe him, but he hurt me, shattered my heart to pieces. He broke me.

"Klay." I sigh as I shake my head. Tears cling to my lashes. Tears I swore I wouldn't shed for him again. "I can't. You hurt me bad."

"I know, baby girl, but I'm going to make it right. I swear."

"ATF? You knew?" Scout moves toward us, and I see the pain in her eyes from me keeping the truth from her. In all the years we've been friends, I've only kept a few truths from her. This is one of them.

I look down at my lap and build up the courage to answer my best friend. When I look up, the tears are rolling down my face now. "I might've kept some things from you. Yeah, I knew." I nod my head at her.

"We will be talking about this," Scout says, waving her hand between Klay and me. She turns to Thad. "You need to get ahold of Kentucky and find out if he's here, but I wouldn't put it past him. He not only wants to hurt me for defying him but for putting him in prison. He also wants to get even with River for helping me. Vixen would be on his list too. And my Kentucky chapter president. I'll have to call her."

"Scout, we need to get Skyler, your mother, and you into a safe house." Thad pushes toward her, and she holds a hand up.

Clear the room," Scout orders.

I stand up, as does Klay. I turn to make sure she's okay. Scout slightly nods, letting me know she can handle this without me. We head out of the room, and I move toward my bedroom that is next to the office. I have to find out what's going on with Klay.

Klay

I watch as she presses her thumb to the lock of the door next to the office.

"You know those can be hacked." I lean into her body, wanting to make sure every man around knows she's mine. If I could piss on her leg like a dog to mark my territory, I would. "I could sneak in and see how wet you get for me in your dreams." I press my cock into her ass, and she shivers. She still wants me, no matter how much she's fighting all of this.

"Hack my lock and get into my room and it'll be the last thing you do. I sleep with a loaded gun now." She opens the door and steps over the threshold. "Come in. We need to talk."

"Wasn't letting you out of my sight, no matter what you think, baby girl." I step into her space. The room is sparsely decorated, letting me know she's painting somewhere else and probably living somewhere else too. She doesn't stay here often. She flutters around the room picking up things, and I see a shirt I haven't seen in a while. I go to grab it from her hands, but she pulls it back.

"Don't," she says, and I see tears pop into her eyes again.

She drops the other shirts and looks at my T-shirt that I last saw in Pandora. An image of her wearing it as she thinks of me flashes through my mind. Her parents' wedding rings are on the necklace around her neck, lying against her breasts that are full and begging for me to kiss the swell of them. I take her in more. She's lost some weight, gained some muscle, and holds herself as if she's ready to fight all the time.

She brushes the tears away before she slings the shirt at me. "Take it. I don't want it anymore. You lied to me, and I can't handle that."

I drop the shirt and move toward her. I want her to wear it. I want her in all my shirts. I want to be with her always. My scent on her so every man knows she's mine.

"Baby girl, I had to leave for your protection. It was all I could do."

"Bullshit. Was it for my protection that you had that whore on your lap?"

Jealousy, I can work with. I grip her arms and pull her into my body and lean down into her. I release one arm and raise my hand to wrap around her neck. She instantly stills, and her pupils dilate with need. I can control her this way and she knows it. She gives me this little submission even though she wants to defy me.

"That bitch sat down because one of my brothers was being an idiot. I told her to get up as soon as she sat down. I only want one cunt and that's yours. I haven't slept with anyone but you. I've kept my vows. Have you?"

She struggles against me. She tries to get her hands up to smack me, but I press ever so gently on her neck. I can't stop myself. I lean down and brush my lips against hers. She stops immediately, and I relax my grip on her arms. Big mistake.

She yanks back and smacks me again.

"That's the last fucking time you hit me, baby girl. I'll have you over my knee and your bare ass will be pink from my palm," I bark at her, and she moves away from me to a small desk. I see the laptop and watch as she opens a drawer.

"I saw an attorney. I don't care if you have a judge. Sign the fucking papers. I want out. I didn't need your pity then, and I don't need it now." She throws a ream of papers at me, and I see the words "Dissolution of Marriage" printed at the top.

Oh, no, she didn't. My lips tip up.

"Can't. Won't sign this." I grip the ream in my fist and tear it down the middle. If it had been a divorce, it would have been a little different. She can get that uncontested, but she went for the dissolution that they have here in Alaska. "I'm never divorcing your ass, and you're never going to stop being my wife. I told you I had to leave to protect you."

"From what?" She throws her hands up, and I'm on her.

I wrap my arms around her, pinning her arms behind her back, and take her lips again. Her breathing is wild, but as I deepen the kiss, she settles down. I hold her wrists with one hand while the other pulls her up my body by her ass. My hard cock rubs against her.

When she moans, I let her arms go and they wrap around my waist. Her small, delicate hand slides under my shirt and up my back. Her nails dig into my skin, and I'm lost to her. I have both my hands on her sexy ass, and I hike her up higher. She wraps around me, and I'm in motion to her bed. I drop us down, caging her below me as I rub my cock against her pussy through our clothes. I need inside her. It's been too long. She's my siren calling to me, always. She could lead me into the rocks, and I'd gladly follow her.

I pull away from her mouth and move down her neck. Her sweet scent of roses hits my senses and I'm overloaded with need. When I get to her full breasts, I suck, leaving a hickey on the sweet swell. I reach into the top and pull a breast out to get to the nipple. I suck it deep into my mouth, tugging on her nipple ring with my teeth. She moans as she arches and pushes more into my mouth.

"I've missed you, baby girl. I need inside you. Need to mark you as mine again."

Her hands slide up into my hair and her grip tightens. She pulls my hair to pull my head back. "Get the fuck off me, now, Klay. I'm not going to fall for your bullshit again." The venom in her voice has me pulling back. Her gray eyes spark with anger, and I realize when I told her I needed to mark her, it must have set her off. A second later she confirms it.

"You can't mark what isn't yours anymore. You threw me to the curb." She slides out from under my body and adjusts herself, putting her breast back.

"Baby girl, I told you I had to keep you safe. I had to leave for a bit. I worked the case. Rescued those women for you. But as soon as I heard you were in danger, I came to you." I fall to the bed and rise up on my elbow as I watch her. I'm trying to figure out how to get her under me again.

"Danger? Fuck, Klay, I've been in more danger than this. You know what the Handmaidens do. How much danger do you think I've been in doing that? Fucking Phantom could have killed me that night. I was there. I saw some of what he did to Scout before he knocked me unconscious," she yells, and the anger from her never telling me the latter overwhelms me. "It doesn't matter. I'd put myself in the line of fire for Scout and Skyler."

I jump up and slam her into the wall, using my hands to protect her from hitting it hard.

"Don't ever fucking say that. You mean something to me. I love you. I never stopped. I'm never leaving you again."

"You did that already, and well, I did," she spits at me and slips under my arms.

I wonder if she means she doesn't love me anymore, that she stopped loving me. She smooths her hair as she steps toward the door but stops when her cell phone goes off. She responds to a text, and I try to lean over and see who it is, but she keeps it away from me. She leaves the room, and I storm out after her. I watch her approach Scout. They talk for a second while they each take shots of whiskey until I notice Thad walking in the clubhouse.

Scout moves away from her, and River settles into a chair at the end of the bar. An asshole in a cut I don't recognize moves toward her. I start to make my way to her so he knows she isn't available. Thad and

Scout talk for a bit before she looks over her shoulder toward River.

"Jinx, you got this?"

"We got it," I say as I wrap my arm across her.

Scout smirks at me as she sees the guy too. I shrug. What can I say? No man is going to lay claim to my woman.

River continues to take shots, and I'm fairly certain she's either trying to push me off with the drinking, or she's going to use that as an excuse to sleep with me. I want to sleep with her. I want to feel her wrapped around my cock again, but I'm not taking her while she's drunk.

Hours later River is stumbling around the clubhouse and laughing as she talks too loudly. The idiot from earlier has another chick, so I've been able to calm down and watch as my girl lets her hair down. I've had enough when Ginger tries to talk her into sitting with another guy. I glare at her. I'm going to have to set her straight. I know my wife hasn't told anyone about our relationship status, but I'm going to make it clear very soon.

I walk over and grip River around the hips. I spin her, and she almost loses her balance. I plop her over my shoulder and take the short walk to her room. I have to let her down when she starts protesting.

"P-Put me down. I'm having fun. It's-It's not like

we're married or something," she slurs, and others around us laugh. I lean down next to her ear.

"Oh, we are fucking married alright, baby girl. Now let me in that room. Right now."

She smiles up at me, and I know she's thinking she's getting lucky. As soon as we are in the room, she starts to unhook her top, her breasts spilling out.

Fuck, this is going to be harder than I thought. I remove my T-shirt and pull it over her head when she drops her jeans. My girl has definitely lost some weight. I need to get her eating again. I haven't seen her eat much tonight. She's drank a lot but not eaten. I should leave her to go take care of Trigger, but I promised her I wouldn't leave. I check the cameras that I installed around the property to see him lying out in the midnight sun. I'll just take her with me later when she sobers up. I wonder if she has a car we can drive.

"I want to fuck," she slurs as I lay her on the bed.

I pull my gun and knife and set them on the nightstand before I drop my jeans. I climb into bed next to her in my boxers.

"Not tonight, baby girl. Let's cuddle. I've missed feeling your body next to mine. And hearing your little snores."

"C-Cuddle. What are you gay?" She doesn't argue about snoring.

"You know I'm not. Now lie down."

She tries to fight me, so I lie on top of her and wrap her up in my arms. My thick cock is hard as a rock between us. I can feel the heat coming from her core, and I just want to plant myself deep inside her, but I'm here for the long game. I need to win her back. I know if I sleep with her now, she'll use that she was drunk against me. She settles into my naked chest and instantly relaxes. I roll off her and lie next to her with her wrapped up in my arms.

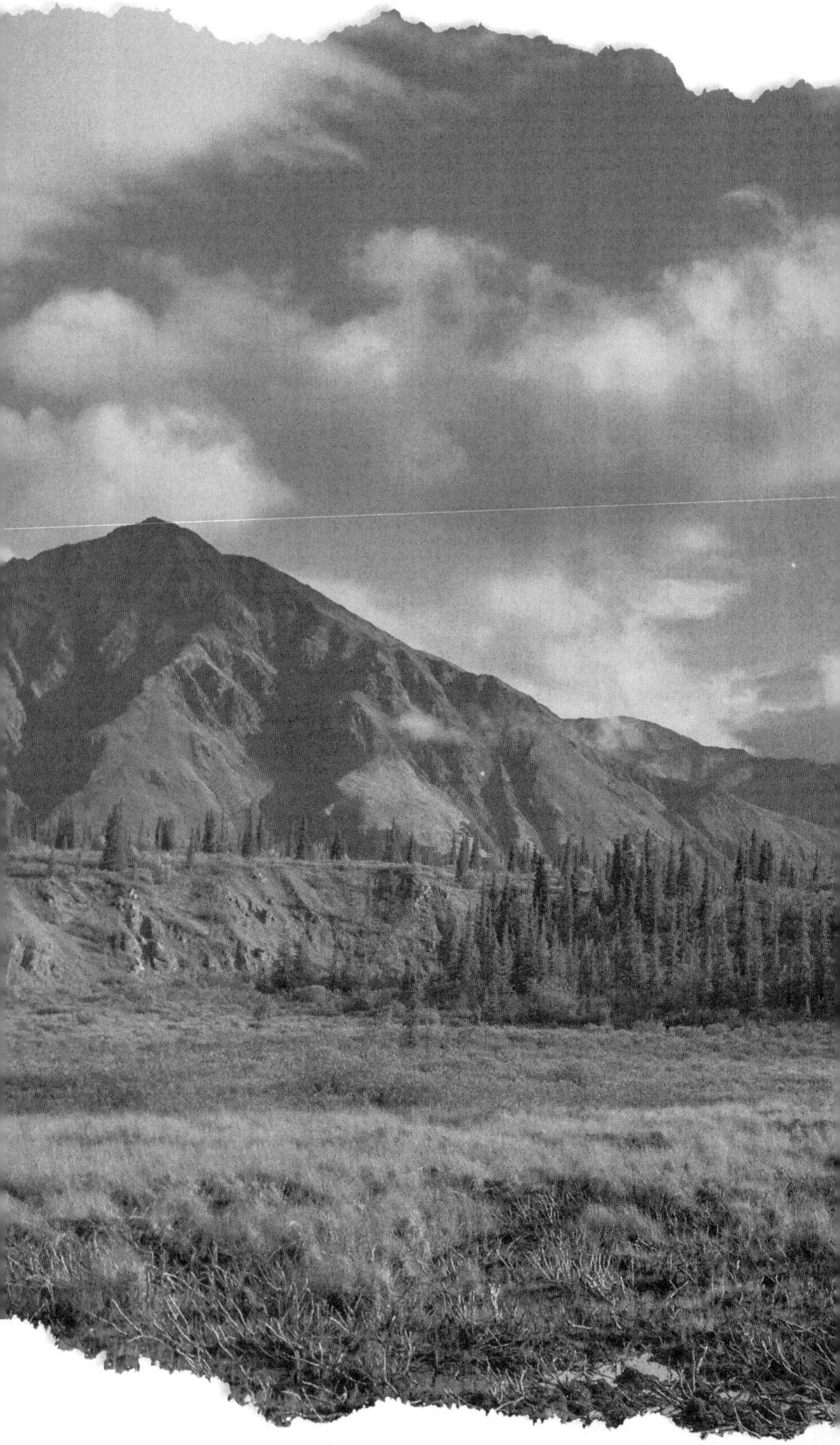

FOUR
RIVER

My cell phone buzzing has me grabbing for it. I woke up an hour ago and took a shower. I look at the man practically naked in my bed. I'm not fast enough, and he's up standing next to the bed with his gun at his side. I hold up my hands.

"Whew, it's just me. My phone went off."

I watch as his body relaxes. It makes me wonder what he's gone through in the last few months. He was jumpy before, but not like this. He slips his jeans back on and grabs the T-shirt I wore to bed. He smells it before he puts it on.

"I don't stink." I defend myself.

"I was smelling your roses. Don't leave this room," he orders before he steps into the bathroom.

The door closes, and I wonder if I have time to flee but decide against it. I want to know what he's really up to. He didn't fuck me, and I threw myself at him last night. He just held me so gently. I heard him tell me over and over he loves me and he won't leave me again.

When he steps out of the bathroom, I notice his hair is wet down, and he takes my hand.

"Where to?"

"Riddler's office," I tell him, and he leads me toward it.

I see the gun at his back and the knife on his hip. The chain that holds his wallet. His muscles bunch as he moves, and my eyes drop to his sexy ass. I want to rub my hand across it, but I can't go there.

"Why the fuck do we need to get up so fucking early?" he says from the doorway.

Scout is at the gun safe arming up. Thad is standing there with her. She texted me that Thad wants to take the kids to the Golden Days parade. I haven't been since I was in middle school. My mom took me the last time along with Scout and her mom. It was one of the things we liked to do together.

"You don't need to come," Thad barks at Klay. It's going to take a bit before they get along. It might not be ever because I can tell Thad isn't sure if he wants to trust Klay.

"You know we are going to a function that will have hundreds of kids?" Thad tells Scout as we stand there. I don't show him that I have a gun at my back too. It's a habit now to carry it.

I look down at what I'm wearing. Thank goodness I dressed in something to go out and about in. I'm in jeans that are distressed in spots and a halter top with a black lace tank underneath that hides my black bra. I've got on heeled black boots and will grab my leather jacket with my cut when we head out.

"You know I don't go anywhere unarmed. Just like you." Scout turns back to Thad and smiles at him.

"Fine, let's go. Dylan will meet us there with Ryder." Thad goes to grab her hand. I guess that answers my question if she's going to ride.

I don't invite Klay, but I feel him behind me as we move out to the garage. I head for my classic Indian motorcycle that's similar to Scout's. I notice that Frenchie gets into Thad's truck along with Skyler and Scout. It's just Klay and me on bikes, so we both ride behind them. We find parking downtown and walk toward Second Avenue, where the parade path goes past. Klay takes my hand as we walk, but I shake it off when we get into crowds. He puts his hand at my back.

I wish I could draw a more definitive line between us, but I can't. I want him close still. I crave his touch. Thad's friend, Dylan, is standing with some chairs along the curb along with Ryder, Thad's son, who runs up and hugs Skyler first then Scout around the legs. I watch as she rubs the boy's back. He's already gotten under her skin, and she likes him. I don't blame her. The little guy is cute and craving the attention of a woman or mother figure.

Us girls sit in the chairs, while the guys help the kids collect candy and enjoy themselves. I watch Klay with Skyler and my heart thumps harder. I want a child with him. No, wait, I wanted a child with him. I can't think of him in the present tense. He's not trustworthy enough. He already broke his word when he left me. There can be nothing that he couldn't protect me from with us being parted.

"So, you aren't letting him eat crow, I see." Scout smirks as she nods toward Klay. "He's good with the kids."

"Yes, he is," Frenchie adds in. I point at both and twist my head as I cock it and raise a brow.

"Don't tempt me to knock you both out. He's eating crow. I told him we are no longer together."

Scout starts laughing, and the guys turn to look at us.

"Stop it. Okay, I tried. He told me I was his and he would keep proving it." I hate confessing this and won't look them in the eye. I want to be tough and badass, but I feel like when it comes to him, I can't be. He makes me feel feminine and needy.

"He cheated on you," Frenchie says. "I mean Ginger saw him with another woman."

"He says that she sat on his lap and he kicked her off it. That one of his brother's thought he needed cheering up."

"Ginger did say she didn't stay there long, so maybe it's true," Scout says.

My ponytail whips me in the face as I shake my head hard. I hold up my hand to stop her from talking.

"Do not be on his side. He could have done so

much more than leave while I was sleeping." I stand up and move behind the chairs and away from them. I catch Klay watching me, and he turns to put Skyler down off his shoulders and walks toward me.

"Baby girl, are you okay?" He starts to pull me in, and for just a moment, I let him before I pull back.

We stand there as Thad and Scout decide what to do now that the parade is over with. They decide to go to the Children's Museum.

"I need caffeine." I can't keep up the pretense without it now.

"We can go get some," Klay offers.

"There's a nice café right down Cushman," Frenchie says as she points.

"Then let's go," Klay says.

It's determined that Dylan will stay with Scout, Thad, and the kids. Klay, Frenchie, and I will head to the coffee shop. I decide to get Scout a drink because I feel bad for getting mad at her.

We are heading back from the shop when we hear an alarm and see people streaming out of the museum. I drop the drinks into the bin next to me and take off running. I hear Klay behind me, but I only have one thought.

Protect Scout and Skyler.

We round the corner along the side of the building, and I watch as Thad is running ahead of me. Blood is dripping from the side of Scout's head, and she is screaming and crying. She's stumbling, and I pump harder to get to her. Thad tries to calm her, but she isn't calming.

"My baby. She took my baby," she cries out in shock and panic.

"Give her to me," I tell Thad, and he hands her off to me. I look her deep in the eyes. The pain of losing Skyler is killing me, but I need Riddler right now, not Scout. I need the ruthless woman I know is inside her. The one who will do anything to get her baby back.

"Sorry, sis," I say before I slap her across the cheek. I watch as she calms instantly and her eyes clear.

She pulls away and is in Thad's face instantly.

"Monica just kidnapped my daughter. You better pray you get to her before I do."

That fucking bitch. Thad's ex-girlfriend has been terrorizing Scout since high school, and now she's gone too damn far.

Scout turns back to Frenchie and me as she pulls her phone from her pocket. I move next to her and look down at the text message.

> **KEYS**
>
> Kid finally got back to me. Motorcycle man had this tattoo on his wrist.

The picture on the screen causes me to see red, and I spin away cussing as she holds the phone up for Reaper to see. He has a deadly calmness to him. We all know that tattoo. It's one of Phantom's.

"I knew he was here," he barks.

"What?" Thad asks, and Scout puts her phone back in her pocket. We know that Keys, our hacker, didn't get that image by legal means, so we can't let Thad know about it.

"I just got confirmation that Phantom is here. We need to get to the compound and get ready. He'll want me, and I'll gladly give myself up for my daughter."

Klay

I hear Scout's words, and if it were my woman, there would be no way she would be giving herself to him for whatever reason. I understand that's her child, but no fucking way would I allow it.

Thad storms over to stand next to her after issuing orders to his trooper friend, Dylan. I watch them because I know what he's going through. Memories of what River and I went through with Crazy last October go through my mind. Him wanting to fight her. I had to kill him. I have no regrets for my bullet in his brain.

"You are fucking not giving yourself up for *our* daughter," he barks at her. "I won't lose my daughter and the woman I love in one swoop." He kisses her hard on the lips and lets her go. He starts moving toward Dylan's truck when he stops and looks at me. "You make sure she doesn't do anything stupid. Her life is in your hands until I come back. Take her and Ryder to the compound," he orders me, and I just nod because that's all I can do. I'm fairly certain he knows that River and I are married. It's all over my official records as a way to protect her, and if he ran a background check on me, he'd see it. He knows I'll protect his woman because it would hurt my wife if something happened to her.

Thad and Dylan take off with Scout yelling at Thad's back that she doesn't take orders from him. Scout pulls out her cell phone and places a call. I stand there to protect her. I know River would want me to, plus I made Thad a silent agreement.

"I want a location on the fucker working with Phantom," Scout says to the person on the other end of her call, and she moves toward the motorcycles. She's got Ryder in her arms, and I can tell she doesn't want to let him go. She's on the war path for her daughter, but I have a feeling she'd destroy everything for him too.

Scout quiets as the person on the other end starts talking. Her gaze cuts to Frenchie. Minuet "Frenchie" Gagnon is one of the youngest women in the Handmaidens. Frenchie is who I suspect River and Scout killed for. I haven't told River yet that is why I left her. I had to make sure it wasn't investigated. I won't lose my girl. I'd fight anyone to keep her.

"Frenchie, take Ryder and go to the compound.

Guard him and my mother in my place. I want Keys, Poison, and Badger backing you up. Make sure Scarlett arms them up. Lock it down. You know how. No one in or out but a Handmaiden." Scout is in full-on Riddler mode. The club president is issuing orders and securing her family.

Frenchie doesn't question her. She nods and moves toward Thad's truck.

"Please bring my sissy and daddy home," Ryder says and hugs Riddler.

River gasps and holds her hand over her mouth. I take her into my arms, and for once she doesn't fight me. She melts into my side.

"Okay, got it. What else?" a voice says after Riddler puts her phone on speaker. Pings chime from both Riddler's and River's phones.

"Jinx and I are going to get the fucker to tell us where Phantom is hiding. Reaper is with us. I want Vixen, Rivet, Scarlett, and Ginger on standby in Fox. I expect he'll call me and want to do a trade. I'll need my bike, some chaps, and lots of weapons. You heard I want you there directing us all."

"On it." The line goes dead, and Riddler looks at both of us.

"Sorry, Jinx, I'm on your bike and you're riding bitch with one of us. We are heading toward Badger Road."

"Get on, baby." I point at my bike. It's my new Harley V-Rod with Ape hangers and an extra-long seat for a passenger. I can't ride the bike I did in

Pandora. It has too many memories. I brought it to Alaska with me though. It's in my trailer. River's bike doesn't have a bitch seat, so she'll be more comfortable with me.

"You promise me you'll keep her safe," River says from beside me after I get on.

I look her in the eye and give her the same promise I did so many months ago plus more. "Your family is safe. I'll do everything in my power to protect them. I gave Thad my word, but you should know I'd do this for you." I hand her the helmet I got for her out of my saddle bag as she climbs on. We turn to Riddler when we are ready and take off following her out of town to the south.

It doesn't take us long to get to an area past the Army base. We turn down a side road and follow behind Riddler as she pulls up to a trailer. It looks so out of place amongst the houses. Riddler is off her bike and pulling her gun from her back. I'm parked and up the stairs behind her as she kicks the door in. I hear a girly scream and see a guy sitting in a chair with a game controller, playing on his computer. He has greasy hair, and his clothes are rumpled and look dirty. The guy jumps up and practically faints when he sees me duck my head to step in behind Riddler. I stand there with my arms crossed over my chest. My cut is on. My tattoos are on display, and I raise my inked brow as I wait for him to answer Riddler's question.

"I want to know where Phantom is hanging out. Where is he having you take the girls?"

"I can't," the guy whines. "He'll kill me." He shakes as Riddler grabs him and presses her gun into his chin. I'm not going to stop her because I don't have a badge right now and he helped Phantom cross the line. You don't bring family, especially kids, into it.

"He just kidnapped my nine-year-old daughter. I'll kill you if you don't tell me. If you do, at least you'll live." She digs the gun into his chin more.

"You'll take care of him?" he asks her, like it makes all the difference in the world. Duh, dude she's going to kill him for taking her kid.

"Yes." She doesn't hesitate.

"Fine."

He gives her the directions. She drags him from the trailer and toward a compact car.

"Reaper, Jinx, follow along," she orders as she pushes in through the driver's side.

River moves to her bike and jumps on. I do the same to mine and we take off again. This time we head back toward Ptarmigan Falls. I make a quick call while we are heading out. Rivet doesn't like helping me, but she does it anyway because I tell her it will help Riddler. The next call is to Titan. I have him research the area with satellite imaging so I can get a better idea of where to park and where Phantom is staying. A plan is forming in my mind as we go.

We pull up to the weigh station in the small town

of Fox, and I stop my bike. I watch as Rivet nods to the bed of Riddler's truck, and I move toward it. I hear what's going on around me, but I'm focused on the things I asked her to bring me. I see the five-gallon bucket that I'll use to get rid of the proof and the long gun that I'm borrowing from her. I would have stopped at my place and grabbed mine, but we don't have time. The meet is set. Thad will be pissed at me, but this is the only way to stop Phantom. I hate that we have to use both Riddler and her daughter as bait to get him to come out, but if I didn't choose to go with her, she would have done it on her own.

I watch as Riddler puts her chaps on. She's working hard not to show anyone that she's upset or worried. I move to River's side when I have everything loaded onto my bike. I hate that I'll have to hump that heavy ass five-gallon bucket while I move through the tundra and brush, but I'll do what's necessary for these women. I pull River away from the group.

"I love you. I'll be back, I promise." I kiss her, taking the kiss deep before I drag her with me to my bike. Once I'm on, I let them know I'm leaving and kiss River again hard. "I swear," I tell her as I take off. I won't let this go sideways and not return to my woman. Fate be damned. That fucking brooch and its curse isn't going to stop me from getting our forever.

I have the pin drop on my map of where Phantom wants to meet Riddler. I've already figured out where

I'm going to park my bike and head there. Titan came through for me.

It takes me just less than thirty minutes to get to the lodge where Riddler is supposed to meet Phantom. I pass it and continue to where I'm going to park my bike. I get off and strap the gun along my back and then grab the bucket. I move through the bush to where I think Phantom will actually be. Titan is able to get current satellite imaging of the area. I have the location of the field with some good intel on an approach.

Another thirty minutes pass with me slogging through the hills and trees. I cross a small creek when I hear a gunshot. I know they are just on the other side of the tree line. I move into a position that has me coming up behind them. I leave the bucket as I shoulder the gun and watch for the perfect moment. Phantom and Riddler are wrestling around and fighting.

Riddler is on her knees in front of him. I'm about to take the shot when she nails him in the crotch, making him fall to his knees. She turns to her daughter, who is tied to a tree behind her. I take aim, and as soon as Phantom holds the gun up, I fire. Riddler's daughter screamed right before I took the shot, so I'm hoping she's okay. I grab the bucket and sling the gun back over my body. I pull my side arm and move through the trees toward them. Riddler is so confused as she's still looking for the bullet in herself and her daughter. My phone pings, and the message is read into my earpiece. It's from Titan, telling me that Thad is almost to the lodge and there is a grizzly making its way toward us.

"We only have a short time. Your man will be pulling up to the lodge in about ten minutes." I drag Phantom to the tree where he had Riddler's daughter tied up. She's in Riddler's arms crying. I need to get control of both of them so we can get this done.

"Grab the bucket. I saw a grizzly moving this way," I order Riddler. "Little Bear, go stand over there and don't look." I use Skyler's nickname. I don't tell Riddler that I have eyes in the sky who saw the brown bear. It might be a carnivore, but it's also an opportunist and will take someone else's kill if it can.

Riddler drags the bucket to me. I pull her knife from Phantom's shoulder and ignore him as he starts stirring. I lift the bucket and Riddler helps me dump the grease over his head and down his legs. This will really attract that bear.

"You killed my brother for that bitch Jinx. I'll kill her next." He threatens, and it takes everything in me not to punch him in the face. "That cunt will die along with these two."

That's it. I swing and clock him in the jaw. His head lolls back as he falls unconscious. Riddler and I move off toward Little Bear. Between the grizzly baring down on us and Thad, we don't have much time. I circled around for a while to be able to approach under cover, but I know where to head to get out of here fast.

When we get to the creek, I rinse out the bucket completely and clean off our prints. I pick up Little Bear, knowing we are running out of time. I start moving faster.

"This way. It's quicker." I point to the trail, and before we know it, we are on the roadside. I continue to carry Little Bear and watch as Scout is slowly starting to fade. She's been hit several times, and her adrenaline is dumping fast.

"Daddy," Little Bear yells, and we look up to see Thad pacing in front of the lodge.

Thad runs to us and yanks his daughter from my arms as he takes Scout into his arms too. I wait until the ambulance shows up before I start huffing it back to my bike. We heard Phantom's scream a little bit ago but ignored it. Then the police radio sent a message about the woman, Monica, who kidnapped Little Bear. She thought if she got rid of both her and Riddler, she could have Thad. That's why she was working with Phantom. She didn't know how truly dangerous he was.

Stupid bitch didn't know that they have Thad's heart, and he couldn't replace them. It wasn't until I had River myself that I understood that. No one will have my heart like she does. I reach my bike and secure the long gun to the side of it. I'll replace it for Rivet and destroy this one before the police ask for it for evidence.

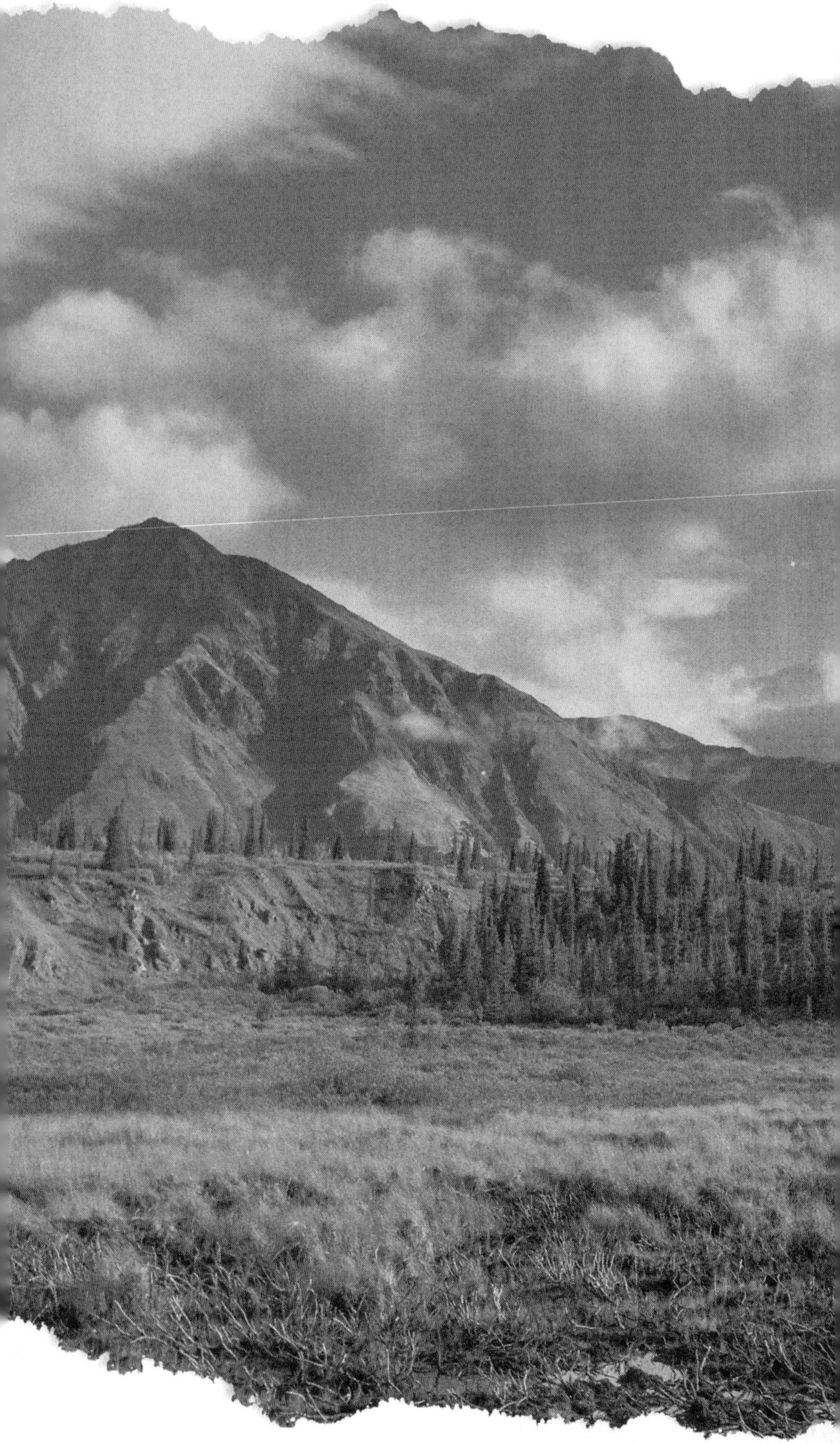

FIVE
RIVER

We pull up on our bikes to the lodge and I see Scout, Skyler, and Thad, but I don't see Klay. My breathing becomes faster, my heart starts pumping harder, and I'm hearing everyone as though I'm in a tunnel. The panic attack is racing up on me.

"Where is he?" I demand as I walk up to the back of the ambulance Scout is in. I want to hug Scout and Skyler and make sure they are okay, but first I need to make sure Klay's still here.

That he didn't get hurt.

That he's alive.

That he didn't leave me again.

As soon as I hear the deep, throaty pipes of the Harley, I know it's him. He comes around the corner, and before he's completely stopped, I'm on him. I throw myself into his arms and his wrap around me. He's kissing me and I'm crying.

"I thought you were gone."

"I'm here, baby girl. I love you," he growls as he continues to hold me close to him.

"I couldn't survive losing you again."

"I'm never leaving you, Wife," he tells me softly as he looks me in the eyes. He wipes at the tears and holds me tightly as he kisses me deep and thoroughly.

We escort the ambulance to the hospital, where Scout is treated and released.

"Come home with me. I want to talk to you."

I can't deny him, and I nod. After Thad assures me he'll take care of Scout and Skyler, I follow Klay to a place off Old Steese and Chena Hot Springs Road. When we pull up, I hear a dog howling. He smiles, and I look between him and the house.

"Trigger is here?" I ask as I take off for the door.

I look into the window and see the big bloodhound. He's as excited to see me as I am him. He's jumping around, and his tail is wagging furiously.

"Oh, my baby boy, mama wanted to meet you," I coo to him through the door. He jumps up on the door and starts whining.

"Get down, you dumbass," Klay barks at him.

"Don't talk to my baby like that."

When Klay told me about his dog when we were in Pandora, I couldn't wait to meet him. I've wanted my own dog for a long time. Rufus is Skyler's dog, and he wants to be by her side always. I thought I had a dog, and then he was ripped from me, just like Klay had been. As soon as Klay has the door open, I push my way inside, and Trigger is on me. He pushes his big body against mine. I sit on the sofa, and he licks my face and presses into me.

"Okay, boy, back off. My girl," Klay orders, and Trigger steps back but immediately sits on the floor near my feet.

Klay sits next to me, and I turn to face him. I slip my leather jacket with my cut off and toss it to the recliner next to the sofa. He tosses his jacket and cut to land on mine.

"Klay, I'm not sure where I want this to go." I try to be honest with him. "I don't know if I'm ever going to trust you not to walk out on me again." He pulls me across his lap so I'm straddling him.

"Baby girl, I'll do everything in my power to come home to you. I wouldn't have walked away from you in Pandora if it wasn't for the fact that I had to save you. I couldn't risk your safety, and I never will. I don't know how Thad handled today, but I remembered what it was like having Crazy after you." He leans in as he pulls me into his lips, and we kiss. His tongue slides between my lips and along my tongue.

Every time he kisses me, it's like coming home. I feel like I've been asleep for months, and for the first time in a long time, I'm awake. He's everything to me, and I can't fight this feeling right now. I rake my nails along his scalp, and he groans. He twists, and I'm lying with my back on the sofa and he's over me.

"I love you," he says to me, and I bite my tongue. I can't give him the words. I'm scared. I'm drowning in my life without him in it, but I'm so scared to trust him. "I understand, baby girl. I'll make it right." He lifts my tanks up and pulls them over my head. "Keep them there." He keeps my arms over my head with my shirts wrapped around my wrists. I'm at his mercy, and I want that. He flicks the button on my jeans and peels them down my legs. When he gets to my boots, he unlaces them and tosses them over toward the door.

I bite my lip and watch him as he takes me in. I try not to squirm, but I can't stop it from happening. He rips my thong from my body. I'm about to complain, but he throws my leg over the back of the sofa and slips the other to the floor before dropping to his knees. His head falls onto my pussy, and he starts licking me as if he's starving for me. He sucks my clit into his mouth, and I arch my back. My hands move of their own accord to bury in his hair. He stops and looks up my body.

"Put them back, baby girl, or I'll stop."

I can't speak. I nod and do as he tells me.

My hands go back over my head. He continues licking me and taking me higher. I'm about to go off when he pulls back. I whimper when he stands up and starts stripping. I take in his body as each part is revealed. He's even more muscular than he was before. His abs tighten when he bends down to take off his boots. I watch them flex as he stands back up, and I almost drool.

"Like what you see?" he asks when I lick my lips.

I look at his impressive cock standing at attention for me. He kneels again between my spread legs and lifts my body and impales me on his cock. He's kneeling and I'm straddling him. We both moan at the tight feeling. It's been so long, and I've needed him so much. I've wanted to feel him just like this.

I start moving. My arms are wrapped around his shoulders as I brace and lift myself off him to slide back down. He flexes his muscles and deepens the penetration. We are both working, and I'm heading toward that orgasm, feeling like it's going to overtake everything in my body. Klay wraps a hand around the front of my neck and squeezes ever so slightly. Everything in my body clenches, needing the orgasm he's going to give me. He's the only partner I've ever had that knows I like to be choked without me having to tell him. It's as if he knows my body better than I do.

Klay releases my neck, and I almost cry. He reaches behind me and unhooks my bra then pulls it off my body. He then starts licking and sucking on my breasts as we continue to move together. When he sucks my nipple deep, biting it, I go off. Everything in my body locks up, and I scream so loud I know his neighbors can hear me. He grips my waist and starts moving me up and down on his cock as he continues to pump into me. He's taking me higher and deeper. He moans, and I hear my name on his lips when he finally comes, setting me off again.

My nails dig into his back, and his hands grip me tight. I fall forward onto his shoulder and hold him tight to me. I want to give him those words, but I'm scared to say them again and have him abandon me. So I hold on to them and bite my tongue.

Klay

I stand and carry River up to the second-floor bedroom, where I lay her out on the bed and take her again. This time I take her fast and hard. As I'm deep inside her and I know she's ready to come, I grip her neck again and she orgasms instantly, pulling me over the edge with her. We didn't use a condom. The last time we were together, she was on birth control. I don't care if she gets pregnant. That's what I want, her tied to me in every possible way. She already has my name. I need my ring on her finger again and then I need my baby in her belly. Thinking about her ring, I look at her naked finger and anger boils through me. I wonder where it is. But that's okay because I got another bigger one for her to wear now.

She falls asleep in my arms, and I hold her tight. I know we still have a long way to go. She hasn't told me she loves me. She still doesn't know why I really left her, and she doesn't know that she could be in more trouble than just Phantom. She doesn't know why I came to her now. The amount of danger she is in.

Titan found evidence that Snake is making his way northwest. I'm scared that he knows she's here and he's coming for her. Even though Titan cleared Anderson, there could be more like Drawer out there. I know Drawer is on the take, but what if someone else is too? What if the whole department is dirty?

River cries out in her sleep. I wrap around her tight in my arms, and she calms instantly, letting me know that subconsciously her heart and body still trust me. It will be convincing her mind I'm not going to leave her that will take time.

After a few moments, I release her body and take care of Trigger. I lock up the small house before I climb back in bed with her. Again, without her knowing, I take pictures of her so that I can always have this moment too. The moment she gave herself to me again.

Wrapping myself around her body, I fall asleep secure in the knowledge that she is mine and will always be. I almost smile because she doesn't know she'll never be able to escape me. That if I can have this with her, she doesn't hate me as much as she'd like others to think.

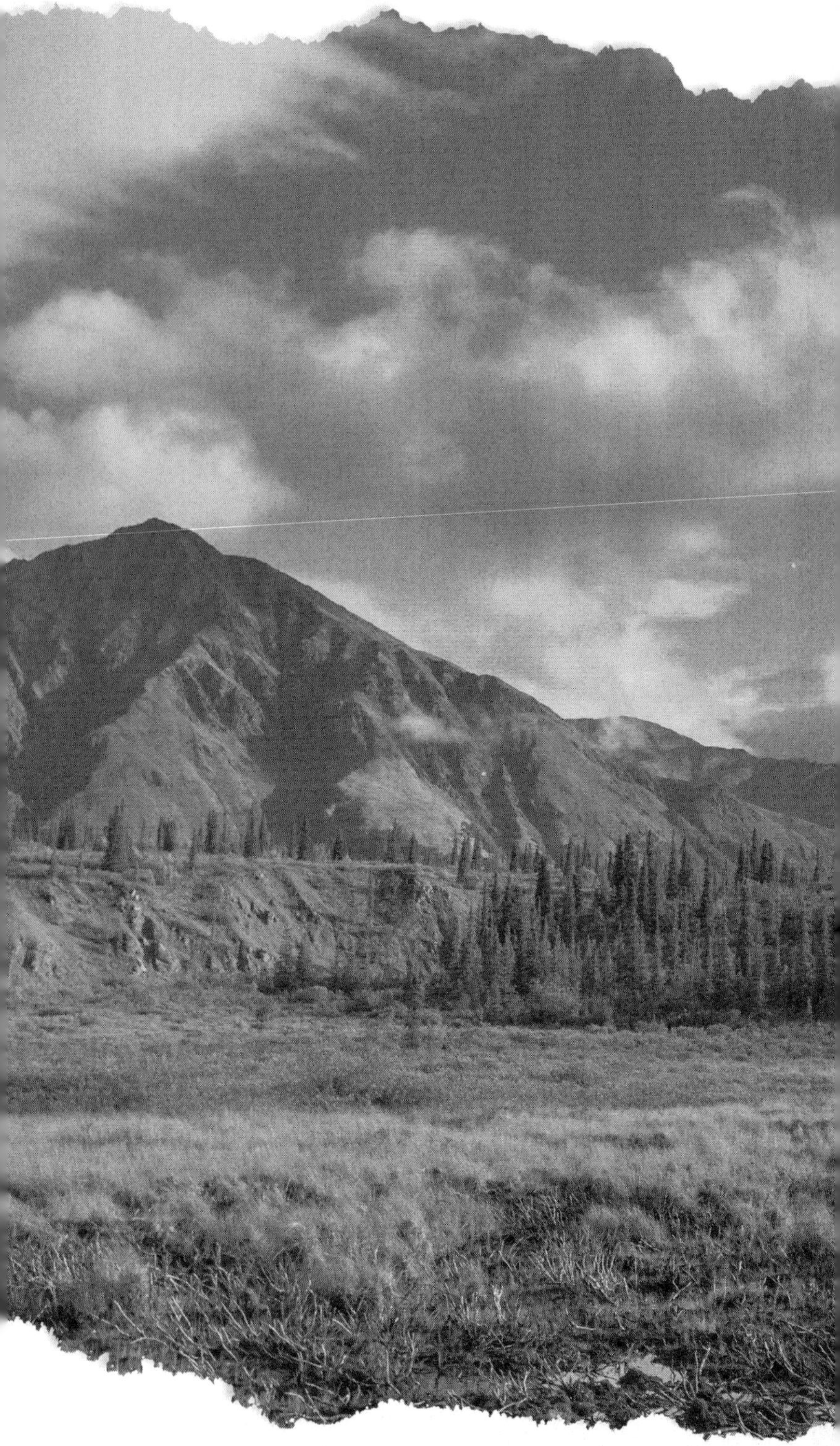

SIX
RIVER

I come awake feeling warm and rested like I haven't felt in months. My body also aches in places it hasn't in a long time. That's when I notice Klay's large arms wrapped around me. I look down and see the tattooed hands of my husband. He's got one arm wrapped around my upper chest and collarbone and the other wrapped around my belly, his large hand splayed across it. Reality hits in that moment.

What the fuck was I thinking?

I come up off the bed so fast that it startles Klay, and I'm looking for my clothes. I then remember they are downstairs.

"Baby girl, what's wrong?" he asks sleepily, and I turn to look at him.

He's all rumpled and sexy. I want him again, but I can't. I remember why last night was a huge mistake when I feel his cum leaking between my legs.

"Fuck," I groan as I rush for the bathroom.

Realizing there isn't one upstairs, I almost trip over Trigger as I try to get downstairs. He jumps up, anxious and pacing, looking around for what's causing my panic.

I grab my jeans and see Klay's T-shirt. I remember he ripped my thong off. After I pee and wash up, I step out of the bathroom. I look around and find my bra on the side table.

"Baby? What's going on?"

I look over to see Klay leaning against the counter. He's got his jeans on, but they are still unbuttoned. He doesn't have a shirt on, and his ankles are crossed at his bare feet. He's sexy, and again I have to shake my head.

"This was a mistake." I throw my hands up and stomp over to the table to get my bra.

"Mistake," he growls, and I realize he's right behind me. I swing around and he's right there. I forgot how silent he moves and how fast he does for such a big guy.

"I can't do this. You broke me, Klay. I'm not the same woman you walked out on." I give him every excuse but the real reason. That I still love him, and I'm scared. That I could be pregnant because I went off birth control.

"I'm going to keep proving to you, over and over, that I don't intend to leave you. I did it for your protect—"

"That's it!" I hold up a hand to stop him. "What if

I'm in danger again? Are you going to leave me again?"

"No. Never again. It almost killed me being away from you. I couldn't focus on the case because I was worried about you. Plus, I'm taking care of the people who threatened you." He tries to take me into his arms, but the words he said keep playing through my head.

I push away from him and pull my jacket out from under his then grab my boots.

"People? Who threatened me? If you know, shouldn't I?" I sit on the chair and get my boots on. When I look up, he's dressed too and ready to go. "Where are you going?"

"With you. Told you, I'm not leaving your side." His eyebrow arches, and I look him up and down.

"No, I need some time. I can't do this. I..." I pause for a moment and think of the words I need to tell him. "We can't do this again. I'm not on birth control anymore. I don't want to risk it."

He's shocked, and I rush for the door and slam it in his face before he can follow me.

I jump on my bike and spray gravel as I twist it around and take off. He's rushing down the stairs, headed for me. I watch in my mirror and see him standing there pulling out his phone. I'm glad he's distracted and not coming after me, but I don't settle down until I'm on the highway heading out to Ptarmigan Falls.

I turn at the crossroad that makes up the only

intersection in our small town, taking the gravel road leading away from the city and to the east. I know this road like the back of my hand. I grew up not far from here. It's where my parents' house is and also where one of the two neighborhoods that make up the majority of the population of Ptarmigan Falls is located. I pass the houses and driveways as I head further away to the five acres and see the large house in my view. I'm focused on getting to my paints and trying to deal with the fact he didn't tell me everything again. Maybe I'm the distraction I thought I was, and he only wants to protect me because I'm in some imaginary danger.

That thought has me slowing down as I pull into the driveway. He said people. Phantom is dead, but he still said people. Phantom wasn't out of jail when he left me. Who else could be after me? Snake?

I throttle down my bike and hit the button on my key chain that opens the door. An explosion and ball of fire come racing at me. My body is flying back before I can even react. I let go of my bike to cover my face from the heat. I kick away from it, and that's the last conscious decision I make.

Klay

It takes me only a moment to realize I don't need to rush after her because the trackers I put on her bike and in her jacket last night are active. I take the call from Titan. The Handmaiden's hacker, Keys, have found his feeds. He says he had to do some quick thinking to get her off his trail. But he found out my girl has a piece of property.

"Trigger, load up," I holler at my dog as I open the back door of the Escalade and then lock up the house before we take off.

I watch the dot turn off the road on my display. I'm not sure where she's headed, but I bet this is the property Titan just told me about. I take the turn five minutes behind her. She won't be looking for my truck but my bike. I'm on the remote dirt road, passing about half a dozen houses sitting back off the road, when the truck is rocked from an explosion. Dirty gray smoke is in front of me, along with flames that go high into the sky. I hit the gas knowing this has something to do with my girl. It only takes me seconds to get to the area.

The house is fully engulfed, and I dial 911 as I'm approaching. I suspect we are out of the fire service area here, but I'm not sure where my girl was when the explosion happened.

I slam on the brakes when I see her crumpled body lying against some trees off to the side. She wasn't in the house. I open the door, and the smoke and the heat of the intense fire hits me. My body doesn't still because I have to get to my wife. I slide to my knees and pause to take in everything before I touch her. She has blood on her face. Her helmet is still on. Her neck is aligned correctly. Carefully, I reach out and check her pulse.

"We need an ambulance," I bark into my earpiece that is attached to my phone. Trigger whimpers and curls up next to her. "I know, boy." I try to reassure him, but I don't know what to do. River's pulse is shallow and thready. I know not to remove her helmet until her neck is protected.

The house rocks a couple more times, and I'm lying over the top of her, sheltering her from the debris when fire and ambulance all pull up. The single engine only has a couple men on it, and I realize it's a volunteer department. They rush to control the fire from spreading, but they don't stop the structure from continuing to burn. It's a hot, intense fire, and I realize what that means. It was sabotaged.

When the medics make it over to us, I hear screaming. I look up to see Scout rushing toward us. She falls to her knees at River's side, but I don't move. I won't leave her side. The moment I let her out of my sight, she was hurt, and I can't let that happen again. I'll do everything I can to protect her. Even if she hates it. I don't know if this is a delayed attack by Phantom or if this has something to do with Snake. My phone has been ringing in my pocket. I know who it is, so I ignore it.

"We need to transport her," one of the medics says.

They have a collar on her and her helmet off. She has marks on her face from not wearing a full-face helmet, but a bucket style one. There's a gauze pad over a cut on her forehead. She still hasn't regained consciousness.

"I'll go with her. I'm her medical power of attorney," Scout says, and I look up at her with fire in my eyes.

"I will go with her. Any medical decisions that need to be made will be done by me."

"You're just her boyfriend, you can't do anything for her."

"I'm her husband," I growl and watch as Scout's head whips from me to River.

"Since when?" Her grip tightens on my girl's hand.

"Don't hurt her." I nod to where she's practically strangling her fingers. "Since October thirtieth. We got married in Pandora."

"Oh my God." Scout rears back. "She didn't tell me." She starts to shake her head. "No, it's a lie. She wouldn't keep that from me."

"She did. Want proof?" I'm angry and stand as they lift River onto the gurney. "Ask him." I nod to Thad. I hate that I'm throwing him under the bus, but I will do everything to protect my wife.

"It's true, Sunshine." He goes to pull her back

when the paramedics move away, and I stay at their side. I toss my keys to Thad.

"Your turn. Watch our dog, Trigger." He nods, and I climb into the back of the ambulance with the medics.

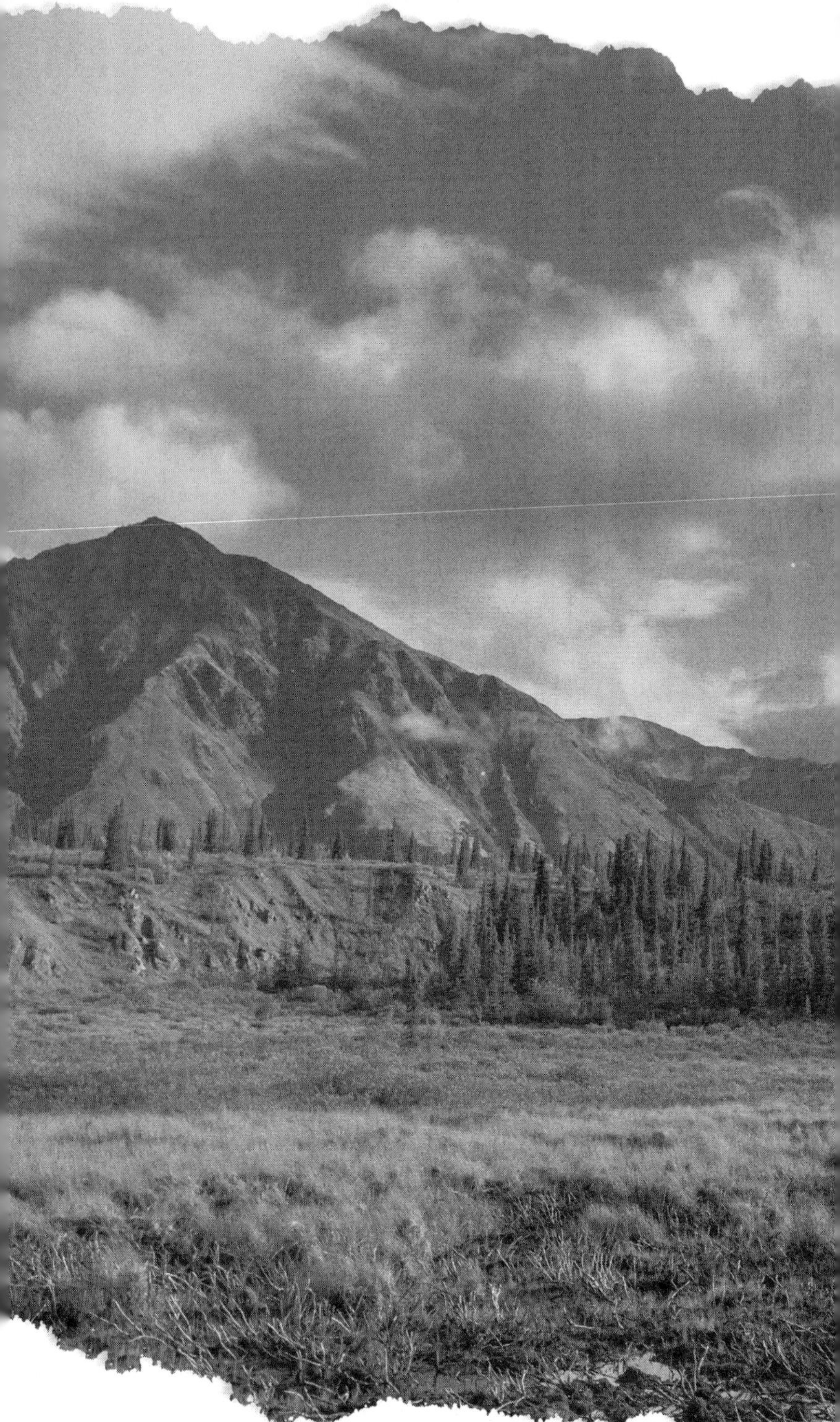

SEVEN
KLAY

The beeping of the machines fills the silence, but it keeps me from going completely insane. She's been unconscious for several hours now. She has bruised ribs at her back from hitting the tree. She also has a brain injury that the hospital is monitoring to make sure not too much pressure builds up. The latter is the most concerning right now. As she lies in the bed, all I can think about is the fact I almost lost her. I look over to see Scout lying across Thad's lap. They followed the ambulance with Trigger in their truck, mine was blocked in.

It's too early to tell if she's pregnant, but just in case, they're are monitoring the meds they give her. I hold her hand in mine and look at the bandages wrapped around her wrists where her gloves didn't protect her skin from the fire. She must have put her arms up to shield her face.

The fire marshal is saying the fire was caused by a

fuel leak at the heating oil tank, but something doesn't sit right with me. It was too intense and too perfectly timed. Keys is pulling up surveillance footage of the property to see if she can find anything.

My phone rings again, and I answer it this time. "Yeah." My voice is gruff and filled with my emotion. I drop my head to the side of the bed and know he's going to be pissed.

"What the fuck, K, you didn't answer. I almost put a BOLO out for you?" Titan barks into the phone, and I know Thad and Scout can hear because they both sit up and watch me.

"I'm okay, but River is in the hospital. Her house exploded." I give him the brief details, knowing he already knows because he has me under surveillance. He always has eyes on me, even when I was overseas.

"I know what the fuck happened. What I don't know is why you couldn't pull out your phone and send me a message to let me know you were okay. Fuck, K, I've been worried sick about you. Don't get me wrong, I'm worried about R too, but damn it, brother." He huffs, and I hear the exasperation in his voice.

"A, I'm sorry. I was focused on my wife."

I like that he included River in using just her initial. I know it's habit for him so that he doesn't give away our real names with his employer. He won't ever be able to walk away from them permanently. Because of his talents, they will always keep him under surveillance or working for them.

"K, she'll be okay. I already looked at her medical file. But you need to know there is a lot more going on than a fucking gas leak or whatever they are calling it. I have the footage. Their girl isn't going to be able to pull it."

"Fuck, A, are you pissing in other people's Cheerios? Let them do it."

"No, she's family now, and I'll protect her, just as I do you." I can't argue with that.

"Okay. Keep searching and let me know." I get ready to hang up.

"He crossed the border ten days ago," Titan says, and I sit up so fast that Thad jumps up and puts Scout behind him.

"What?" I stand up, keeping my hand on River's. "He's here?"

"Yes. I can't get out of here for a bit, but as soon as I can, I'll be there."

"Fuck." I throw my head back as I crush the phone in my hand. When I look down, I find River's eyes are on me. She's awake.

"Klay?" she says in a scratchy, soft voice.

I drop to her side and take her hand and press my forehead to it.

"I'm so sorry, baby girl. I tried to keep you safe, but Snake is here." I want to destroy everything in my path but her. I want to cling to her so he can't hurt her.

"Is he the reason you left me?" she asks, and I

don't care who's in the room with us. I give her the truth she desperately needs.

"No. There is a man at the agency who I believe is out to get both of us. He…" I pause, trying to figure out how to say this to her. I know deep down she's going to be mad at me for not trusting her completely, but I had to protect her. That need to make sure she's safe overrides everything in my body.

"The man who threatened me on the phone?" Her voice croaks, and I reach for the water cup. I put the straw to her lips and watch as she sips before I continue. It gives me time to collect my thoughts more before I continue.

"Yes, baby, that's the man. The last night I was with you, he threatened to have you arrested." I see her gearing up to fight. "Now wait." I hold a hand out to stop her. "Yes, he threatened to have you arrested for answering my phone, but that isn't what made me walk away." I look over to where Scout is sitting. I'm not sure what she's told Thad of their past. "Maybe I should tell you this by yourself."

"No. Anything about her, I want to hear." Scout stands up and moves to River's other side. "She doesn't need to keep secrets from me regarding you."

River holds her hand and looks at her with tears in her eyes.

"I agree. I'm sorry I kept things from you, Scout." She turns to look at me again. "She knows everything about me," River says, and I look to Thad.

"Don't get your panties in a twist," I tell him

before I continue. "I met with Deputy Chief Drawer before we went to Pandora. He was really jonesing for the Handmaidens. He wanted me to infiltrate your club and find information on you." River starts to sit up. "Lie back, baby girl, I told him no. I didn't use you. I swear. I love you and didn't marry you out of pity or as a job. I married you to tie you to me permanently. Got it?"

Tears spring to her eyes, and I lean down to kiss her mouth gently.

"I love you. Everything I've done is for your protection," I tell her, but I can't stop what's going to happen next. "Drawer had sent me a copy of an arrest warrant for you for suspicion of murder." I watch her face closely. Her eyes stay focused on me. With her head injury and everything she's been through, I suspect her emotions are running high, but she doesn't give anything away.

"I haven't murdered anyone. I've thought about it. I've wanted to badly, but no, I never did."

"What about the man who tortured Minuet?" I use her real name instead of her road name. River's eyes flick to Scout, who slowly turns to look at Thad. "He's been missing since you recovered her. There are rumors he was murdered by a couple of women matching your descriptions. I looked into it so that I could bury it to protect you. I couldn't let you be pulled into the politics of my job because he wanted to use you as collateral."

"I didn't kill him. Neither did Scout." River takes

my hand in hers. I see the pain register on her face as she flexes her wrist, but she doesn't stop. "I wanted to kill him. I'll honestly tell you it came close. God, I had my gun in his mouth, but I didn't pull the trigger," she confesses. I look to Scout next.

Scout shakes her head. I've wondered if it was her, but her words stop me cold. "I was there. I let River take the lead on it. She saw what Minuet looked like. She saw the look in her eyes before I pulled her away and held onto her. She didn't kill him. I didn't either. It was so close. It was a line we were prepared to cross, but we didn't. That would have been murder, not justifiable, because both River and I are trained, he wasn't. He was unarmed. We left him broken, beaten, and very much alive in that cabin in the woods. We didn't kill him."

"Well either he's dead or he's playing dead. I know what that's like. The man I suspect Drawer to be working with is part of the Aryan Brotherhood. I thought I had him one time. He went by the name Lucifer. He was a gunrunner who several people saw run into a building that exploded. I think he got out. I think he's still alive and pulling all these strings, including Snake's." I pause as I figure out how to tell them about Titan, what information I'm willing to give out. "A friend, a brother of mine, found the footage."

"Then we need to protect River. He won't come after me, but her, he will," Scout says, and I nod.

"Yeah, he'll do anything in his power to get her."

"That's why you left me. You didn't trust me." River's voice cracks, and I gently take her face between my palms.

River

I look into Klay's eyes, scared he's going to confirm my worse fear. How can he not trust me? I wanted to kill that fucktard for hurting Minuet, but when the time came, I couldn't do it. I left him a message though. I cut off one of his nuts. I didn't tell Klay that. Neither did Scout. That we keep to ourselves.

"I love you. I didn't care if you killed him or not, I couldn't have you going to jail because of me. If you had killed him, it would have been justified because he raped and tortured your sister. A young girl who couldn't defend herself."

I take a deep breath when he finishes talking, and my eyes grow heavy. As I drift off, I wonder if I'll ever be able to trust that he won't walk away from me again. Now, I'm in more danger than before and yet he's staying by my side.

. . .

The next time I wake up, only Klay is in the room, and he's sleeping in a recliner next to the bed. His big body dwarfs the chair. He looks so uncomfortable. I wish he'd just go back to his place and stay, but my heart thumps harder thinking he wants to be with me and won't leave me. He's keeping his promise not to leave me.

"It seems impossible that he fits into that," a voice says, and I turn too fast, causing my head to swim. I see a nurse through my blurry vision. "Relax, it's just me. I'm your nurse for the day." She introduces herself and proceeds to check my vitals then says she'll bring me a tray of food. After she walks out, Klay rises from the chair.

"Thought she was never going to leave." He leans down and kisses my forehead next to the bandage.

I don't know what my injuries are yet, but I don't care. I'm just glad I'm alive when it hits me. The loss is so great I open my mouth to cry out, but nothing comes. My chest tightens from the pain.

"My parents' home," I cry, and Klay carefully pulls me into his body and holds me as the pain intensifies. "It's all gone. Everything." I scream out as I think of everything that was in there.

"I know, baby. I know. I'm so sorry." Klay holds and rocks me as he tries to comfort me. "I'll rebuild it. I'll do whatever you want."

I finally hiccup my last sob and look up at him as

he holds me. His words wash over me, filling the holes left in my heart.

"I don't want a house like that anymore," I tell him quietly, my voice scratchy. He holds the straw to my lips, and I take a deep gulp, refilling my system with the essential moisture I just streamed out on his shirt. "Please don't leave me again."

"I swear I won't." He slides onto the bed and lies down with me, holding me until I fall back asleep.

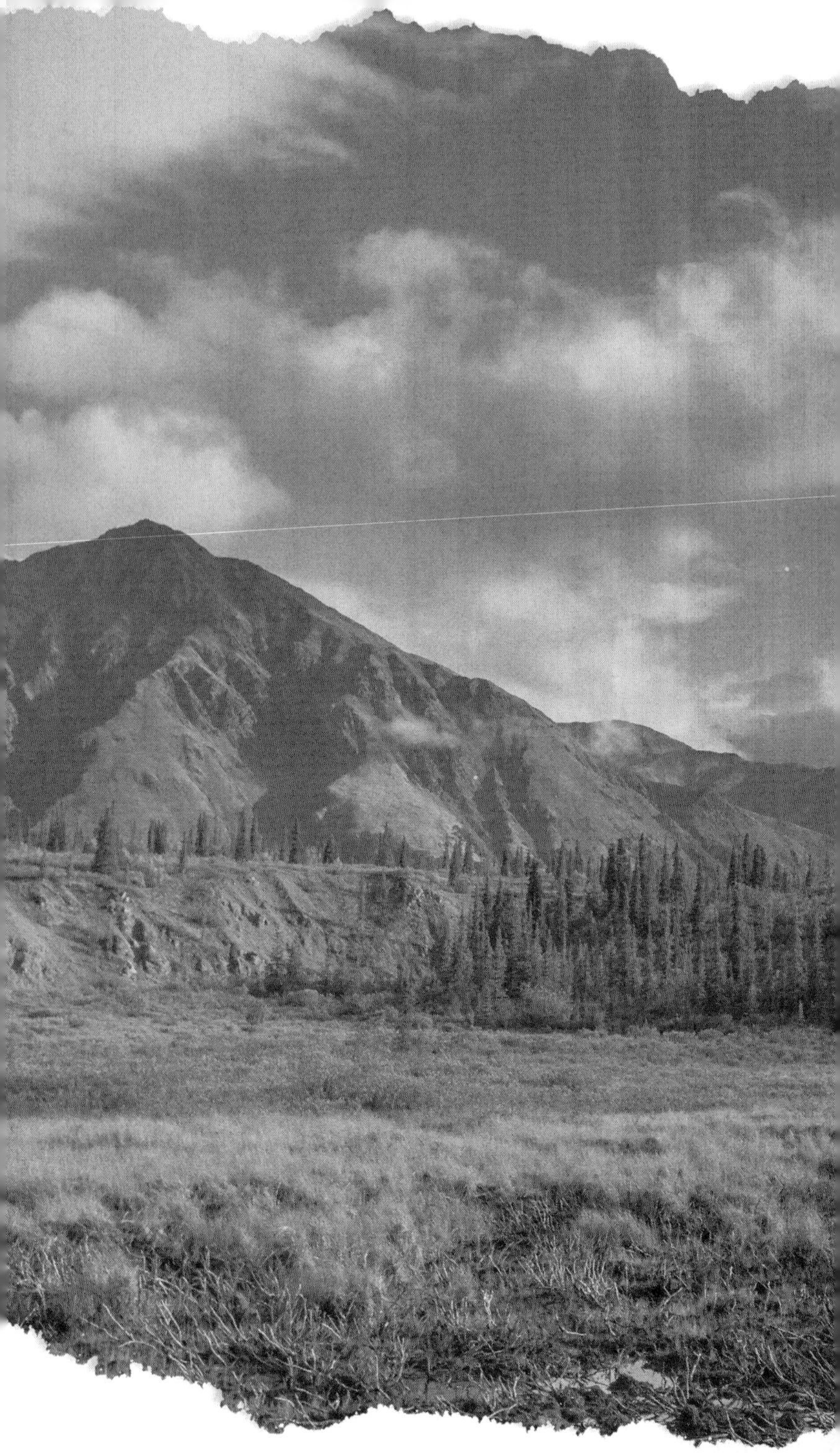

EIGHT
RIVER

I've been home from the hospital for only a day. I was in there for four days. Klay hasn't left my side. He's currently sitting on a stool as I carefully paint a pinstripe down the side of the custom tank for a bike Scout and I are working on together. Nobody wanted me to come back to work, but I couldn't stay away. I needed to do something. I lost so much, and I haven't even seen the damage yet. Klay says he'll take me out there this afternoon if I want. I do, but then again, I also don't. I don't know if I want to see the destruction.

My bike was also destroyed in the explosion. I'm glad I kicked it away from myself when I did.

"Want to go to the fair with me next weekend?" Poison asks, stepping into the shop. She's the bar manager of the saloon next door that Scout owns, and she's also Thad's little sister. Vixen nicknamed her

Poison because she comes up with some sick ass drinks that will fuck you up.

"No, she shouldn't go," Klay answers for me, and I turn to look at her as I set my brush down.

"Yes, I'd love to. We can walk around and eat our way through it." I chuckle and she full on laughs.

I remember Poison when she was a kid following us around when we were in high school. Now she stands before me with deep purple hair, a curvy body, tattoos, and facial piercings. I don't judge because I'm tattooed and pierced myself. But it's a far cry from the blonde who was upset she didn't have boobs at thirteen like the other girls in her gym class.

"River." Klay's voice has that intimidating quality that causes most people to give into whatever he wants, but not me. He's been so overly protective of me. I need this, and so does he.

"I won't ride. You can drop me off, or I'll take one of your rigs."

"You can take your car," Scout says, walking through the shop. "I can pull it around and we can run some quick diagnostics on it."

I thank God my father's car was stored here and not at their place. It wasn't destroyed in the explosion. This is the only thing I have left of them other than their wedding rings. Calmly, I stand up and pull the key chain out of my pocket. The key is there, as well as my wedding ring from Klay. When he sees the ring, he smiles. I'm sure he thought I got rid of it. I couldn't do it. It's like the brooch to me. If I get rid of it, I'd have bad luck.

I walk around the building, and I know he's following me along with Scout. She's practically bouncing as we go. She loves playing with muscle cars, and my dad's is one of her favorites. I haven't touched it since we came back. I know her dad kept it tuned up and good while I was gone. It's just an excuse to play with it for Scout. When we get to the back of the building, I know we have an audience, and part of it bothers me, but I know they are here to support me. I unlock the storage door and slide it open. Not only is the car in there, but so is another one of my riding bikes and my dirt bike. I'm glad I didn't have everything at the house because it would all be gone now. In the back corner are a few of my paintings that I didn't have at the house.

Reaching for the cover over the car, I slowly drag it back. My wrists and ribs are still tender. Klay helps pull on the other side. As each part of the car is exposed, I start to feel a bit faint. It's been so long.

"Fuck, baby girl, this is sexy," Klay says as the car is revealed.

I'm staring down at the fine stripping along the hood edge. The filigree style calls to me, and I drag my finger along it as memories flash through my mind. My father helping hold my hand steady. Him leaning over me as he lets go and watches me do it by myself. I don't realize I'm crying until I feel Klay wrap his big arms around me. I lean back into him as I smile.

"He was so proud of me for how steady I was. He said that it was a skill that not many are born with, to free hand that good." I chuckle as I remember him bragging to so many men about it.

Klay kisses my neck. "He loved you and knew you were talented, baby."

I nod and then pull away from him to open the door. The scent of the leather mixed with the old car hits my nostrils, but I swear that even after all these years I can smell my father's aftershave. I slide into the seat and look across the swooped hood to where Scout is standing. Her eyes are shiny from unshed tears. I insert the key into the ignition and turn it. The car fires up instantly. All the barrels fire and rumble. A thrill causes my heart to thump, and then I hear the Bon Jovi song playing in the cassette recorder and can't stop the full belly laugh. I pull the door closed and drive the car out of the garage. Everyone moves aside, and I drive to the front of the shop.

"Now that's a sight I haven't seen in a long time," Thad says after I park outside one of the bays for Scout to check the car out. "Loved this car almost as much as I loved Levi's truck." Thad brushes his hand up the back and over the top.

"That's fucking sexy," Klay says as he pulls me into his arms.

"Yeah, she's pretty hot. Maybe later I can take you for a spin in it." I turn in his arms and bat my lashes at him as I smile. I thought it was going to be worse, but instead, it felt like coming home.

Scout pops the hood, and sure enough, Levi kept it in tune. Everything sparkles under the hood. I'm not surprised that it almost looks better than the last time I saw it.

"Dang, Daddy took away all my fun." Scout pouts, and Thad chuckles as he takes her into his arms.

Thad is primarily taking some time off but had to go into the station today for a meeting. He doesn't want to leave her side very much after everything that happened. I'm glad he was there for her when I was in the hospital. Scout doesn't care for hospitals much after she spent a while in one after Phantom beat her up so badly.

We spend the rest of the day going through the car so I can drive it until I'm healed enough to ride my bike. Klay wants to take me back to his place early, but I've missed everyone and want to spend time with them. When the saloon opens later, I'm sitting in the office with Scout as she leans back at her desk.

"So, you're giving him a second chance?" she asks me, and I look up from my phone where I was responding to an email. She has a mischievous grin on her face, and I raise my eyebrow as I take her in.

"Yeah. You gave Thad one."

"Oh, I'm not questioning if he deserves it or not. I was just wondering how you feel about other bitches being on him." She chuckles and nods toward the monitors.

I look over, and sure enough, a skank is leaning into my man as he sits at the bar listening to the live band.

"That fucking bitch."

I recognize her as one of the many bitches who decided to start coming out here after Scout reopened the place. Scout rebranded the saloon a bit, and it attracted more locals. But this is one of the crew who used to run with Monica. I'm up and out of my chair and heading for the office door.

"He said he was only going to go out and get a drink." I stomp through the back hall toward the front of the saloon.

"You just got out of the hospital." Scout is rushing to keep up with me.

"I don't fucking care. I'm tired of these bitches thinking they can take our men."

I push past people, and I see the moment that Klay notices me approaching. He looks over the skank's head, and his eyes are dancing with laughter as he holds up his hands palm out to show me he wasn't touching her. I can't stop the anger from erupting. I've needed this for so long. I grab the bitch by the back of her head and pull her back into me as I lean toward her.

"Don't fucking touch my husband," I growl as people around us gasp and the saloon silences. The music no longer playing.

"He didn't say he was into dikes," the bitch hisses. The fucking nerve. She goes to throw her head back, but I push her away from me. "Besides, he said he was into me." She points over to a table, and we all turn. Sitting there is the man who's been trying to get my attention for weeks. The man who I told I wasn't interested in. Klay gets to his feet and starts to move toward him as the bitch turns on me. "Maybe if you kept your man satisfied, he wouldn't go looking for someone else."

I see red. This bitch is skating on thin ice. I feel people move around me and hear the commotion of Klay talking to the other biker, but I'm focused on this skank. You're taught not to take your eyes off a snake when it's coiled, and she is that.

"I keep my man well satisfied. Now leave before I throw you out like we did a couple months ago." She was with Monica when Scout had to politely escort her and the crew out of the bar. I was involved in that, and if I remember correctly, it was this very bitch that I threw out. I look her up and down before I shake my head. She isn't worth it.

I start to turn from her, not wanting to fight, when her fist slams into the side of my head. I fucking took my eyes off the snake, and she struck. I rock on my feet as my head swims in pain. I hear people around me and then my husband's bellow before my eyes clear. I spin, not caring that I just suffered a head injury. The ringing in my ears muffles the sounds around me, and I pull back my fist as I see her eyes flare wide. I punch her hard in the face, not caring about anything but making her feel the pain I am in right now.

Arms wrap around me as I go to hit her again, aimed at her gut this time. It's slow motion as blood sprays from her nose toward me. I'm kicking and screaming at whoever is holding me as I watch her being dragged away by one of Ginger's bouncers. I throw my head back, connecting with someone, and more pain explodes in my head. I'm transferred from the arms into another set as I continue to fight and yell. I don't know what I'm saying or what's going on. A hand wraps around my neck, and I feel the familiar grip as the fingers flex, and I calm instantly.

"You there, baby girl?" Klay's deep voice breaks through the fog.

I look down at my hands covered in blood. People are watching me. I turn my head and see Ginger has a cloth held to her face. Instantly, I realize what I did.

"Fuck. I'm so sorry." I drop my head, upset with what I allowed to happen. As soon as that bitch hit me, I was lost to the pain and took it out on everyone around me.

Ginger scoffs. "It's been a while since someone got a hit on me. I guess you and I need to work out some more. I'm okay. It's not broke." She laughs it off. "I deserved it. I shouldn't have grabbed you."

"No. I'm sorry." I shake my head for a moment, and that's when they all start moving. I'm up in Klay's arms and being carried out of the room. I realize the haze around my vision is me getting ready to lose consciousness from the hit to the side of the head. "Bitch hit me in the temple." My voice sounds like it's coming from a tunnel.

Klay

I'm lying in bed next to her. I stripped her down to only a pair of sexy panties. The sheet is down to just over the top of her ass. She's on her belly. I wish I could take her, but I'm worried about her head and ribs. I can't believe she attacked that woman last night. I understand why she did it. I let that asshole know she was my wife and off limits to him. He tried to say she never told him. I assured him that was no excuse. He backed off and said the woman asked if I was taken and he said he didn't know. He didn't direct her to come after me, she chose that on her own.

When I turned and saw her hit River, I was in motion, but I didn't get there fast enough. Then she hurt herself more by attacking Ginger. She almost fainted but assured me she was okay, so I didn't take her to the hospital. Now she's lying here sleeping next to me. I'm about to get up and head down to make coffee when I notice her body tighten up. She's awake.

As she tenses more, I realize she's going over everything that happened last night. That I had to get her out of the fight by using her kink on her. It was the only thing I could come up with. I made sure it only looked like I was holding her and not choking her. I also know that she knew it was me.

Reaching across the bed, I slide my hand under her body and between her legs. She turns, and I drag her across the bed and onto my body. She wraps around me, burying her head into my neck as I hold her. I can't stop my fingers from sliding against her panty clad folds. She moans, and the sound goes straight to my balls. I hold her against me, still worried about making love to her with her injuries.

"Fuck, baby girl, I want to sink balls deep into this pussy, but I can't yet."

She leans up and smiles down at me as she sits up and presses her pussy into the head of my cock. My eyes almost roll back into my head. I'm about to say fuck it when both our mobiles ring from the nightstand.

"Saved by the bell." She chuckles as she leans over, putting a breast in my face as she grabs the phones. I suck her nipple into my mouth, wrapping my tongue around it as she tries to move her hips to get some friction.

She drops the phones next to us, and I roll her over and rise above her. I look down to see her biting her lip. It's not sexy this time. She's sore, and I know the fight last night didn't help. I push up off her.

"Soon, I'm going to fuck you so hard you'll forget everything." Our phones go off again.

I grab mine and see a message from Scout.

RIDDLER
Need my VP for church.

ME
Give us time for coffee.

I look at River and notice she's texting someone.

"Scout needs me."

"Yeah. Let's get some coffee."

"Yummy, sounds good."

We get up and shower quickly before we head out to my SUV. I adjust my cock in my jeans when I think of how much I wanted to take her in the shower. She reaches across the console and rubs her hand on my thigh.

"I can take care of that on my knees later." She laughs, and I groan. The image of her on her knees the first time she took me almost makes me wreck the truck, which causes her to laugh harder.

When we pull up to the compound, a guard lets us through the gate. I park and walk around the truck to let River out after I told her to stay put. I open the back door next so Trigger can get out. He jumps down and takes off to go play with Little Bear's dog, Rufus. I notice Thad is watching his kids play.

"I'll hang out here, you go to church." I know I

can't go with her, and I figure Thad will want to talk about Snake and the latest issues.

Yesterday was hard on River, both physically and emotionally. I know getting her father's car out of storage wore on her nerves, but I'm glad she did it. The fight, on the other hand, was not only unexpected but shouldn't have happened. I should have stayed by her side instead of going to blast the fucker who's been trying to make a move on my wife. No one knew we were married until recently, and then last night she announced it to the whole damn saloon.

"You can't let her out of your sight either." Thad chuckles as he watches the kids play around.

"Yeah, I guess. Plus, she can't ride yet."

"She was lucky that those ribs weren't fractured like they first thought. But, still, bruises is bad. It's a good thing she wears a jacket with plates in it."

"Yeah, a lot of the Handmaidens wear them. It's a safety feature that more and more motorcycle brands are doing. Even mine has some safety features to it."

I watch his son and daughter play and my heart aches. I can't wait until River and I have this. Thad and Scout only have one child together, but his son isn't treated any differently than their daughter. In the years they were separated, he tried to move on, just like she did. River told me about his ex-wife walking out on him and Ryder. The boy is a cute kid and loves his big sister.

"Hello, Reaper." Skyler walks over and hugs my legs.

"Hey, LB. How are you?" I refer to her Little Bear nickname.

"My mom and dad are worried because I still have nightmares."

I can't believe it's only been a week since she was kidnapped. The kid is too smart for her young age.

I pull her up into my arms. "It's okay. I have them too. I'm glad I got there on time."

"You do?" she asks me, and her eyebrows climb. "But you're a big guy and a fighter like my dad. I heard Auntie River say you were in the military too, like him." I chuck her cheek, and she grabs my hand to inspect my hand tattoos. "I don't want them to worry about me. You and Mommy saved me. I knew she'd come."

"Just because I was in the military and can fight doesn't mean I don't get scared. It's when you aren't scared that you need to really worry. When I was in the military, my…" I pause. I was about to tell her about A. "Well, I had this friend who kept an eye on me. He worried about me too. That's what family does. They worry. And your dad was right there with us. He just was a little delayed."

"Oh, I know Dad would have found me too." She looks at Thad and smiles. "He didn't know about me until a month ago," she says. Too damn smart, this kid. "I knew he was my dad the first time I saw him. He has my eyes." She points to her face, and both Thad and I laugh.

My cell pings from my pocket, and I set her down before I pull it out.

A

> He's on the move to your location. I'm heading out.

ME

> No, stay there. I'll be okay.

A

> Too late. Handler came back clean. Drawer is on his way there too. He's sending some friends.

Just as the message comes through, we hear a commotion at the gate and turn to see several unmarked SUVs trying to get in. The girls start flowing from the clubhouse, and I watch as Minuet walks over to the kids.

"Prez asked for you to come too," she says to Thad.

Together, he and I move toward our girls as agents exit their vehicles. These are federal, not local. I can tell from their attitudes.

"How can I help you?" Scout says as she gets to the gate.

River and Ginger are flanking Scout. Us guys stand behind the group of women. I take in the agent who steps forward. I'm not surprised when he pulls his wallet and flips out the FBI badge.

"Hello, Ms. Keller, I'm Special Agent Colberg. I'd

like to ask you and Mrs. Ulrich some questions about a case we are working."

I go to push past them, but River reaches back and holds my hand. I know who did this and why. I'm pissed. Fucker couldn't let it go.

"Agent Colberg, you didn't have to bring all this for just a few questions." Scout waves her hand at the six SUVs. "I won't answer questions without my attorney. Can we set up a meeting?" She cocks her head to the side.

"We have a search warrant. We'd also like to speak to Minuet Gagnon."

"What is this search for?" Scout asks.

The agent hands her a piece of paper, and she looks it over as he waves to the SUVs to proceed. But the Handmaidens don't move from the gate.

"Agent Colberg, just a moment."

We look up as another car pulls up. I watch as Scout's uncle jumps out and walks over. He must have been at his place instead of in the office, but it is a Saturday. I watch as Joel takes the paperwork from Scout.

"I'm Joel Keller. I represent Ms. Keller and Ms. Schmidt." He pauses and looks over at me. "Sorry, I mean Mrs. Ulrich." He reads through the paperwork quickly and shakes his head. "This search warrant is for a location in Kentucky, not here. You can't search here."

"It's for Ms. Keller's and Mrs. Ulrich's living quarters. They don't live in Kentucky, they live here."

"Yeah, but it's got an address listed and a judge that doesn't have jurisdiction in Alaska. This isn't even a federal judge." Joel chuckles. "Get your paperwork in order, then you can search. As for the questions, you can meet both women at my office on Monday at say ten."

The special agent shakes his head as he rips the paper from Joel's hand. "They are murderers, and you are protecting them."

"Did you find a body to prove that?" Joel only pauses for a moment. "No, you didn't. Get off this property now, and if you accuse them again without proof, we'll sue you for slander." Joel stands his ground with his arms crossed across his chest. People start loading up, and the SUVs all pull away. But the fleeting look I saw on the special agent's face tells me this isn't over. He's working with Drawer.

Joel turns and points at each of us. "You four with me. Minuet too."

Scout's mom, who was working at the café, walks up and says she'll watch the kids. We follow Joel into the clubhouse, and he waves at Scout to take the lead. She heads for her office. When we move into the room, he closes the door behind us.

"First thing's first, River, I'm assuming I can destroy the divorce papers."

I stop at his words and turn toward her.

"I told you"—I pull her into my body and tip up her chin to look me in the eye—"I'm never letting you go. No divorce. No dissolution. Nothing. Only death." I growl each word.

"That can be arranged." She laughs at me with a twinkle in her eye.

"That's not funny right now," Joel barks as he moves behind River's desk, taking over her office.

"No, Uncle Joel, I don't want a divorce any longer." River chuckles again and leans up to kiss me. She'd told me that Joel wants her to call him uncle too because he considers her a niece.

I let her go, and she turns to face him.

"Okay. This is my 'I told you so,' by the way." Joel laughs and then sits down. "Let's discuss this. Thad, I know you don't know anything, but I figured you wouldn't let my niece in here without you."

"Damn straight."

"You know this is my office, Uncle Joel."

"Yes, but right now it's mine. Klay, while you were at the hospital with River, Scout and Thad told me everything. I was at home doing some research when I got this call. That agent is trying to fast-track his career, or he wouldn't have been here so quickly. As for the evidence, they only have circumstantial stuff."

"Why do they want to search here? What would the girls have here?" I ask and look at them.

"There is nothing. They're trying to find other things. Something about proof of illegal means and goods."

"But that has nothing to do with a murder or missing person's report," Thad says, and both he and

I are using our law enforcement training to figure out this angle.

"Girls, I need your alibis. I also need yours, Klay." His words stop me, and I look at him with an eyebrow raised.

"What the fuck does my alibi have to do with this? This happened before River and I met. I can't give it to you. It would blow several agent's covers if I turned that over."

"Your name was on the search warrant too. The agent didn't tell you? They've already searched your old house; it was a rental. Of course, they didn't find anything."

"This makes no sense." I start pacing and notice that Scout is saying something quietly to Minuet.

"We are each other's alibis," River says, and it's then that I realize what is circumstantial.

"They have no proof, just that the girls were all together. That's what they are basing this off of."

"Yep." Joel pops the P, and I can only shake my head.

"It's a witch hunt because they can't prove the DHMC isn't dirty."

"We don't do anything below board unless we have to." Scout moves to the door as a knock sounds on it.

"We have to call this meeting, Uncle Joel, I have other things I need to take care of."

"You girls can't do anything. Don't do it, Scout. If

you break the law, they could come after you and rip open your lives."

"Then I guess we don't get caught." River chuckles.

"Goddamnit." Joel storms around the desk.

"Just be ready with that safe house," Scout says to him, and he nods as he moves out of the room.

I push the door closed behind him and round on the women.

"What the fuck are you thinking? River can't ride."

"I'm in a vehicle, and we have no choice." River squares off with me.

"Baby girl, no." I can't think straight when I don't know the plan or what I can do. Then it hits me. "I'll ride in her place. She can stay here with the kids and Thad."

"I'm not staying." Thad looks at Scout. He's just as pissed as I am. These women that we love keep putting themselves in danger, and it goes against everything for me to not tie mine to our bed and make her stay put. But this is one of the reasons I fell in love with her. Her independence and need to help.

"Frenchie, go get ready," Scout orders.

I watch as she moves out of the room, and I turn back.

"This is club business, not your business. We will do this our way and you won't interfere."

"I can help. And we do this the legal way so that

agent can't use it against you." Thad tries for reason, but neither of them are listening to us.

"You're on leave. What if it was your sister or someone you cared about trapped out there?" She moves into his arms, and I turn to my wife.

"You can't do this. You are barely recovered." I pull her into my arms.

She shakes her head and looks up at me. "Klay, I have too. This is a big deal. I promise that I won't do anything to get hurt. You can wait here, but I have to go."

"Fuck." I throw my head back knowing I can't talk her out of it.

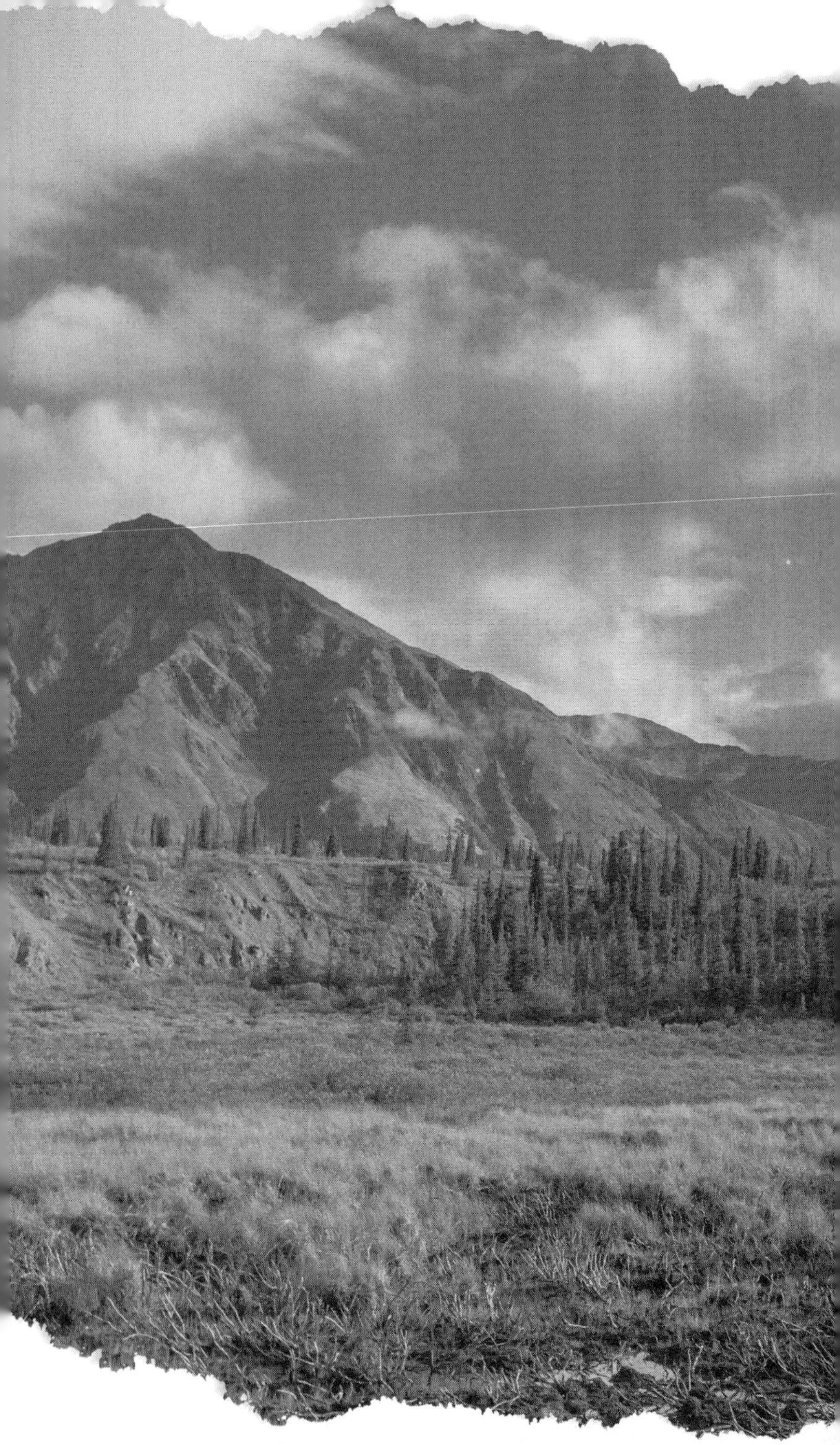

NINE
RIVER

Klay watches me as I climb up into the blacked-out SUV that we own through a shell company. With all the fed after us we decided to change things up. We aren't leaving in a group, and we'll all be going different places, leading them off as a diversion. When the medical organization came to us for help, we couldn't pass them up. This needs to be done to protect these kids.

I blow Klay a kiss and know he's going to try to follow. I tried to talk Scout into letting me be on one of the diversion groups, but those are all bikes. They need the large vehicle to help transport victims.

Keys found the crack house that first attracts the teens and then gets them hooked before it turns them out, pimping them to pay for the cost of the drugs. She's been doing the research and coming up with the plan to get as many out as we can. We've had surveillance on the building for weeks now.

As I head down into Fairbanks, I stay on the highway and get off in the South Cushman area, making my way to where the house is. I don't see Klay's bike or truck behind me, and we haven't had a tail. I move through the streets, passing the house several times before I see Scout, Vixen, and Ginger rush out the door with several young teens. I barely stop the rig and they're pushed into the back.

Because of the addiction issues and the detox, we know they will need medical care. I head out toward the house Joel helped us procure. It's across town off Chena Pump Road. I have the escort behind me of the other bikes, and I make sure I'm driving legally and not drawing attention to us. Those feds have us spooked, but they won't scare us from doing what's right. I pull into the garage and wait in the truck. This setup isn't part of the DHMC. We only got the property.

These people who help here are part of the medical nonprofit organization that helps get teens clean. We found out about them when we moved back up here a few months ago. They'd heard of the Devil's Handmaidens from the Lower 48 and said they wanted to work with us. They help teens get off drugs and out of bad situations. These kids will be taken care of and then moved to a location out of town to recover. Their names won't hit the system to protect them. Then they'll be returned to their homes only if it's safe. If not, they'll be moved out of state to safety. We have to be very careful because most of the teens are listed as runaways. Legally it's kidnapping on our part by taking them. Even if it is to help them. That's where Joel and other attorneys volunteer to help us. They get the teens emancipated or the courts to deem their current home situations as unfit.

As soon as all of the kids are out of the vehicle and the door is secured to the house, I jump out and make sure they didn't leave anything in the back. I then back out of the garage and head toward Ptarmigan Falls. It only takes moments before I'm under escort again. As I'm traveling on the back road heading toward home, I'm pulled over. I know I was driving correctly and not speeding.

I roll down my window and tell the officer I'm putting my gun on the dash. He looks at me and then tries to peek into the back.

"What's up, Officer?" I ask him as I see Klay's motorcycle going past us. I don't know how he did it, but that's the first time I've seen him all night.

"Got a call about a vehicle similar to this being stolen."

"It's a company vehicle." I hand him my license and registration along with my insurance card. He looks at them all and then hands them back.

"Have a good night."

I nod and wait until he's back to his car before I pull out onto the road and continue toward Fox and Ptarmigan Falls. I'm a little shaken up, but I don't let my hands shake until I pull into the garage at the shop and park the rig. I jump out and immediately fall forward, bending at the hip. I take several breaths and try to calm my heart. I've never had this reaction before on a run, but after the explosion and finding out they are looking at me for murder, I'm freaked out.

"Baby." I hear his voice before he slides his hand along my back. I stand up and wrap myself around him.

"I was so scared."

"I know. It's okay."

"I didn't kill him."

"I know that too. I don't know why Drawer is jonesing for the Handmaidens, but I have someone looking into it."

"Okay."

He holds me for a bit longer and then we head out to his place to pick up Trigger.

Klay

As soon as we cross the threshold into the small house, I whip her around and slam my mouth onto hers. I know I shouldn't, but I need inside her like it's the breath in my body. We pull at each other's clothes, removing them. I hear rips and buttons popping, but we are naked and I'm sliding her down onto my cock as we sit on the sofa. She leans back and grimaces in pain, then she leans into me. I wrap my arms around her and hold her close as I move her up and down on me.

"I want you to take me hard," she begs.

I bite her neck and then lift her up. She is standing in front of me, and the edge isn't even gone. I only pumped inside her two or three times before I realized this wasn't going to work. I turn her around and help her get back on my lap with her back to my chest. She slowly slides down my cock and my eyes cross. She moans and cups her tits as her head falls back on my shoulder. With one hand around her waist, I guide her. I wrap my other hand around her throat. As soon as my fingers tighten slightly, I feel her pussy clench around my cock. Pulling me in deeper.

"Baby girl, I'm going to take you nice and slow. I'm going to protect you but give you what we both need. Got it?"

"Yes. Yes, Klay," she cries out as I release her neck so she can answer me.

Over and over, I help her up and slide her back down in a slow but steady rhythm. She twists and moves around until I squeeze my fingers. She sighs and I flex, slamming up into her, giving her a bit of the edge she loves so much. When I feel the flutters along her cunt, I know she's close. My balls are drawing up and I'm ready to blow, but I need her open and ready for me because I'm getting her sweet ass pregnant so she can't go on runs like this for awhile. I slide my finger across her clit and rub it in tight circles. She's about to go, so I give her another squeeze of my fingers. She gurgles out as she comes, her juices sliding down my cock. I slam up into her a couple more times before I release.

"River," I moan her name, and turn her head so I can take her lips.

When I break the kiss, I look down her beautiful, sexy body. I'm getting hard again at the sight of her splayed out across me, but I need her to rest before we do it again. I lift her off and she just moves slightly. She's almost out from the adrenaline aftermath. I wrap her around me, chest to chest, and press her back into the back of the sofa. My body shields hers as we both fall asleep together.

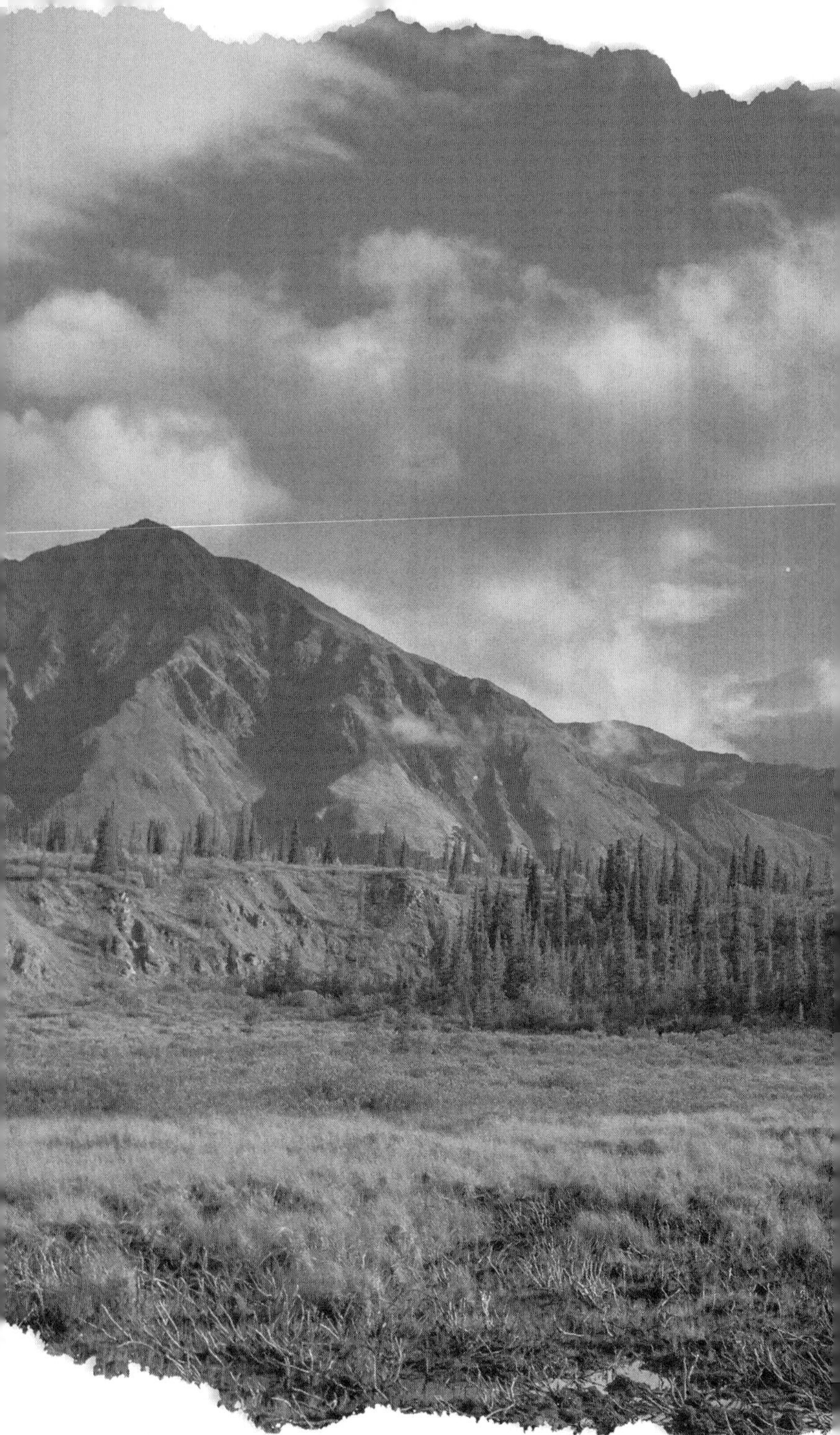

TEN
KLAY

I don't like this one fucking bit. There are too many fucking people around us. She parks the car in a spot she's directed to and smiles huge at me.

"I'm fucking you hard tonight after I choke you on my cock for this," I growl as people move around us toward the entrance.

I don't know how she fucking talked me into this. I was sure that Thad would be on my side and say it's a bad idea. But nope, instead he went along with it, and now I'm stuck going to the fair. It's nothing like the miles of fair in Kentucky, but it's still big for the small town. She told me about the locals from all over the area who come here with their prized vegetables and livestock.

I come around to her door and let her out, and she slides the keys into her pocket. She started wearing her wedding ring again, but now in its place on the key chain is the brooch that she got in Pandora. It's attached to a piece of leather. I've seen some of her paintings. I know she's sure that we have to break the curse on the damn piece of jewelry. I hate it. It reminds me of the shit we went through in Pandora. The only good thing was marrying her, so maybe it's not so bad after all.

It's been over a week since we met with the feds. The girls all gave their alibis, and I referred them to my handler. There are no grounds for the searches, so the feds are sitting back waiting. I can't shake the feeling that something isn't right. I'm missing something. I take a moment to look around us, feeling like I'm being watched. The back of my neck tickles, and the hair along my arms is raised.

"Come on, I want to split a turkey leg with you." River chuckles as we head toward the line for those with e-tickets.

We move through the crowds with my hand tight over hers. She tries to shake me off as she stops to look in booths and the small tents that people are selling goods from. But I don't let up on my vigil of keeping her safe. I swore I'd protect her and that's my plan. By the time we get to the section where the barn is with the animals, I see Thad standing watching over Scout and the kids. When a man moves to stand next to Scout, Thad folds his arms across his chest and stares the guy down.

"Can we play games now? Auntie River and Uncle Klay are here." Skyler points to us as we walk up.

"Rides," Ryder screams, and even with the loud noises around us people turn to look.

"Buddy, tone," Thad reprimands him, and he nods his little blond head.

I've spent the last week talking my girl into not getting back on birth control so we can have a little one too. I want this with her. It's the next progression for us. I have my ring on her finger, and I spoke with a builder who will be breaking ground on a place for us on the compound's property. We have the dog, so now it's time for a baby.

"I want to talk to Scout." River looks up at me.

I finally give in now that I have Thad to help me keep an eye out for danger. We move through the crowds to the rides and games. The kids want to ride a few different rides, and we end up splitting up when they fight over which adult they want riding with them. I walk up after riding the spinning teacups with Skyler to see River and Scout with their heads close together.

"Good luck, man." Thad laughs as he moves to ride the carousel with both kids. I look down at my wife, and she smiles up at me from the bench the girls are sitting on.

"What?" I know she's up to something, and I raise my brow.

She stands and reaches up. "I love when you raise this brow." She slides a finger over my brow tattoo. "It's sexy."

"I'll show you sexy," I growl in her ear so only she can hear.

She steps back and I see the flush move up her body. "How?" She pauses, and I know she's waiting to say more as she bites her lip. I pull her full lip from between her teeth.

"Only I bite these." I lean down to kiss her when we hear the kids yell. I pull my head back, and we turn to smile at them as they wave at us.

We turn back around to see Poison walking up. The fair was her idea, and then she wasn't going to make it due to having some issues at the saloon. But she got it all figured out and is now showing up to spend some time with all of us. All of them grew up together, which makes their bond really tight. This is what I want for my kids. Being a kid who grew up in the system, I want something different for my children. I want extended family close by.

"Hey, Stormy." Scout greets Poison by her real name and pats the bench so she can sit down with her.

"Did you ask him yet?" Stormy asks River, who shakes her head and turns back to me.

"How would you feel about renewing our vows in October so all of my family can be with us?" She looks down like she's afraid I'm going to say no.

I lift her chin up and wait until she looks me in the eye. "I'll marry you as many times as it takes for you to be happy."

"Yes," both Scout and Stormy cheer, and I realize what this means.

"Shit."

"Yep." River smirks at me.

"Girls trip to Anchorage," they all squeal, and I shake my head.

"That, I didn't expect." I look down at her. "When?"

"We were thinking next weekend so that I can get a dress here on time. I might have to go off the rack if the order takes too long." She huffs and I pull her into me.

"Order whatever you want and have it delivered here. We can have it altered if needed."

"I want to try on dresses with my girls."

"I don't want you travelling away from me."

"Come on, let's get some food." Scout changes the subject.

"We will discuss this more," I whisper in her ear, and she nods at me.

"Can I persuade you with blow jobs?" she whispers for only me to hear, and I smack her ass as she turns away from me. She huffs and looks over her shoulder at me.

We get in the food lines. I'm in one for barbecue, and I watch her carefully as she moves with Stormy to a counter a couple down from me where they have turkey legs. They are chatting and having a good time. I turn to look at where Thad and Scout are standing with the kids at a hot dog stand. When I turn back around to look for my wife, she's gone.

"Hey, man, the line is moving." A guy goes to push me, but I look down at him. I step out of line and move to where River was, but I don't see her. It was only seconds. I turned my back for only seconds. I see purple hair in a crowd and move toward it, but it's not Stormy.

"Fuck," I exclaim, and people turn to look at me. I pull out my phone and dial her immediately. "Where are you?"

"Oh shoot. Sorry. Stormy forgot her wallet. We are making our way out to the gate where she came in. I'll be right back."

"No. Get back here and I'll take you," I order her, and I know the moment she's pissed at me. I hear her little growl and huff come across the line.

"I can take care of myself. We are going out the yellow gate." She hangs up on me, and I storm over to Thad.

"Where's the fucking yellow gate? Stormy forgot her wallet, and they are going out there without any protection."

"Shit. I'm coming." He turns to look at Scout and then back to me. I know his indecision and fear.

"Point. I'll go." He doesn't want to leave his family as much as I don't want mine walking around without me.

"That way." He points behind us, and I take off in that direction.

I see the yellow banners flying, pointing out the gate, and my heart calms but only for an instant. A gunshot rings out as my phone starts ringing. I'm running.

River

"I can't believe that man. I've been taking care of myself just fine for years." I complain to Stormy. I'm looking down as I slip my phone in my back pocket when I slam into her back. "Oh, sorry, I was distracted." I look up and over her head to see a man standing there. I recognize him instantly and grab her arm, spinning her behind me as I slip my keys out of my pocket and hand her my phone. I'm hoping she knows to call Klay.

"What are you doing here, Snake?" I hold my keys in my hand when I realize I'm not parked at this gate. Shit.

"You know why I'm here. Now come here," he barks as he cocks the gun in his hand.

I look at the gun and then back to Stormy, who isn't looking at me but at the men starting to surround us. There are six of them, and I know I'm not going to be able to take them all. I know that Stormy is trained, but not as much as me.

"Hey, what's going on here?" a deep-voiced man says.

I look at him. He's got long brown hair that hangs to his shoulders. I watch as he nonchalantly pulls it back and puts it in a man bun at the back of his head. His beard is trimmed similar to Klay's, and his nose is the same. I don't know how I know, but I know he's related to Klay. He's tall, just a bit shorter than him, and built very big. He's got a Drago Defiance cut on that says VP on the chest rocker. He smiles at me, and I pinch my lips, trying to hold in the need to call out to him.

Snake swings the gun and fires. I watch as the man falls, and I scream as I hear Klay's voice coming through my phone. I'm grabbed from behind but fight my assailant off. People have scattered, and it's pandemonium.

Stormy screams and cries out. I turn to see a man dragging her toward a van. I fight to get to her, but something hard slams into my head, making me see stars as more gunshots ring out.

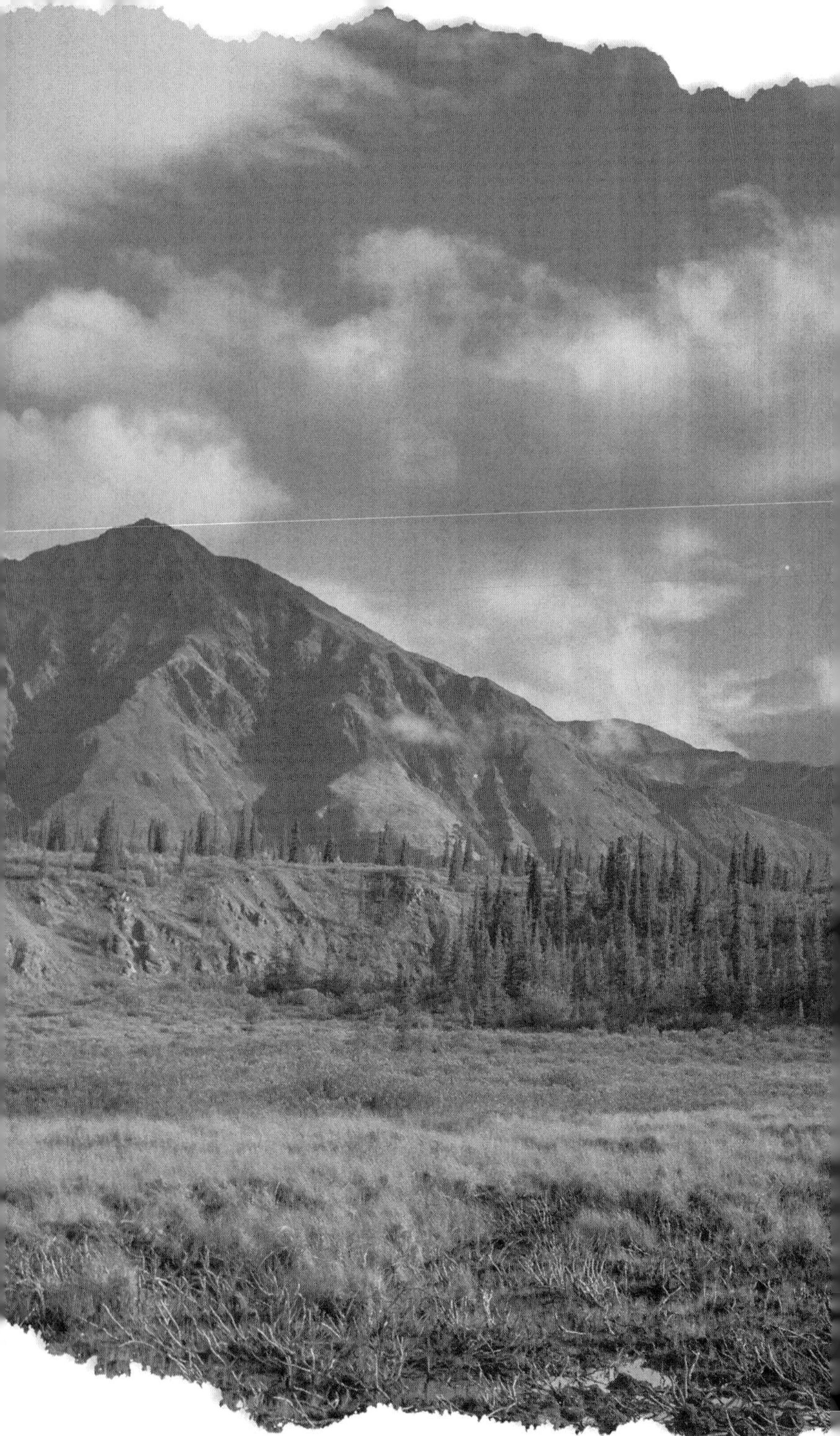

ELEVEN
KLAY

I hear the screaming across the line and then the laugh I'd never forget.

"You'll never get her now. Oh, and I have an appetizer for my main course," Snake says into the phone before the line goes dead. My heart clenches so tight in my chest that I almost collapse. I can't give up on River. I will fight and do everything I can to rescue her.

People are running from the parking lot toward the entrance, trying to get away from the shooting. Women scream, and men try to protect their families. I pull my gun from my holster at my back and shout, "Out of my way. ATF." I'm not anymore, but I'll do anything to get to my girl.

I make it through the crowds to the parking lot in time to see a van rushing away, bumping across the gravel. I'm about to fire at the rear tire when I hear a gunshot. I dive for cover and turn to see Titan standing there with his gun aimed at the van as he fires at the back of it.

"I tried to stop them," he says, and I take in the gunshot wound to his shoulder. "Fucker shot me as soon as I walked up."

"Are you okay?" I move toward him as we both watch the van taking off. "Let's go." I spot my girl's keys on the ground and reach down to pick them up along with her shattered phone.

"Hands up," cops yell, pointing their weapons at us.

We are ordered to set our guns down and hold our hands up. These fuckers are going to allow Snake to get away from me.

"Wait, they…" Thad pauses and then looks at Titan. "They're not the ones. His wife was abducted, but I'm not sure about the other one." Thad quickly identifies himself as a state trooper.

"They fucking took her. We need to go," I bark at Thad.

"Take my bike." Titan tosses me his keys.

As I start to slip River's keys in my pocket, the fucking brooch catches the sun. I flip it in my hand before I toss the keys at Thad so they can take her car back to the compound. Fucking bad luck again. I swear this priestess is a bitch. We need to prove her wrong to break the curse. I'm never letting my wife go.

"No, wait! We have questions," one of the officer's

orders, but I don't stop. They'll have to shoot me in the back.

I take off hoping I can catch up to them. I need to follow them and rescue River.

An hour later I pull into the compound, and I'm pissed as fuck. I lost them, then the cops pulled me over and wanted to question me. I told them to fuck off. If not for Titan and his friends in higher places, I'd be in jail right now.

"Anything?" I growl as I throw the stand down on Titan's bike. He walks up with his shoulder bandaged. He's in a tank top and jeans. His long hair is pulled into a man bun. "Sorry, how's the arm?" I lift my chin toward it.

"I'm fine. I'll have a pretty scar to show off to babes." He tries to make light of it, but I see the grimace on his face when he tries to shrug. He's in pain.

My brother might work for a government agency, but he's not an operative and doesn't get shot at regularly. Even with the MC, he doesn't end up doing many dangerous things. He's built like a brick wall, but that's from working out so he doesn't look like the computer nerd he is. His physique has nothing to do with his job.

"I have surveillance running and facial rec. I ran the plates on the van. Stolen. I also have a few other irons in the fire." He pauses and looks around before leaning in to whisper at me. "She knew who I was."

I lean back and can't stop the chuckle. "She would."

"There is nothing funny about this." Thad storms over to us. "They took my baby sister."

"He took River too," Scout says from next to him.

"I know. This is Titan, he's one of my brothers." I introduce him.

"We've met," Thad says then turns to him. "How did you get out of being questioned? You produced a card and said you can't talk. Who are you with?" he demands, and Titan ignores him, which makes Thad angry. He grabs my brother's arm.

I shake my head because Titan used his connections for himself too. This could be good or bad for either one of us. They could show up here and take over, or they could take Titan back and leave us all hanging. He looks at Thad and I notice they are the same height, just Titan is a bit bulkier. Finally, I see the moment when Titan takes pity on Thad. Something crosses his face, almost like he's in pain and empathizes with him.

"National security," is all Titan says and then turns back to me. I watch as Thad calms slightly. "I stopped and grabbed my gear from your place. She wouldn't let me drive River's car." He points to Scout, who hands me back my wife's keys.

"What else did you find?"

I ask the question as red and blue lights filter

through the yard. We turn to see the feds pulling up. Those fuckers would be on us because of what happened.

"We don't have fucking time for this," I growl as I storm toward them.

"Wait," Titan says, as he races past me.

He hands his phone to Agent Colberg, and I stand there with everyone else listening to the person yell over the line at him. I grit my teeth, wanting this to be over so I can go rescue my wife.

"Yes, sir. I'm sorry, sir. I'll take care of it." He starts to hand back Titan's phone when another car pulls up.

This one is obviously a rental car, and I watch as Division Chief Drawer steps out of it with a smirk on his face. I advance on him, ready to wipe the smile off his face when more cars slide into the gravel driveway. These are large blacked-out SUVs without lights flashing but still have the look of a government agency. Several men in black tactical gear get out and advance on Drawer. One stands head and shoulders over the rest. He has a stocking cap on his head. The guy has to be almost seven feet tall, and that's not all. He's so bulky with muscle, he makes my brother and I look like skinny guys. His trapezius muscles are so large that his shirt looks like it's going to rip at the seams. I wonder if it makes turning his head difficult, but it doesn't seem so as he turns to look at my brother. He gives a slight nod, and I turn to Titan and look at him confused. I flex my fingers, knowing I'll have to shoot this fucker if he comes at me because I won't be able to take him on.

"Marek Drawer?" the big guy asks.

I watch as Drawer's eyes almost bug out of his head, and he steps back, the fear clear on his face.

"Yes, but it's Division Chief Drawer." He straightens his jacket and fixes his tie that is already straight. I know it's a tell. He's nervous. He fears this guy, not only because of his size but because he's unsure what this man represents or who.

"You are under arrest for murder and suspicion of conspiracy against the government," the man says.

Before Drawer can dispute the charges, he's spun around and his face is down on the hood of the car as cuffs are slapped onto his wrists. Drawer was eating paint in the blink of an eye. The big guy holds him down with one hand only.

"I didn't kill anyone. Do you know who I am?" He screams and complains before he's dragged toward one of the cars. Another one of the men in black moves to take Drawer from the big guy, who then walks over to where we are standing with Special Agent Colberg.

"You aren't needed here anymore. We've closed the case on LaRue's murder. His body was found yesterday, and evidence points to him." He points back to the car Drawer is in. He then holds out his hand for the phone. The agent hands it over, and the guy ends the call before he looks at my brother.

"Titan." He walks over and hands the phone to

my brother. "Cronus wants to know when he can expect you home." The man's voice is deep and gravelly, as if he gargles glass. I realize who these men are, and I reach out to stop Scout, who is advancing on them. I signal to Thad, who grabs her back. These guys won't think twice about throwing anyone into Gitmo.

"We need to know where our friends are. You can't take that man if he helped in her abduction." Scout refers to Drawer.

The man turns to Scout and pulls off his mirrored shades. He has pale blue eyes that bore into you when he looks at you. That's what makes him a good operative.

"Ms. Keller, this man doesn't know where they are, but we'll make sure to get as much information out of him later. If we find anything, we'll let Titan know." He turns back to Titan.

"Hermes, just tell Cronus I'm not sure what my plans are yet. I might want to retire." My brother wobbles his head back and forth as if he's considering it. "I kind of like it here." Titan looks around as the wind blows past us. I'm not ready to joke around.

"I need to know where my wife is." I look up at the man, Hermes, who is looking over my head at the women behind me. He looks back down at me.

"Mr. Ulrich, Titan will fill you in on the information we have so far that will not interfere with national security." He turns away from me and back to my brother.

"I'll tell Cronus to get you set up here. You know you can't leave. You still have ninety-nine more years." He laughs and turns to leave but stops and turns back to look over my shoulder. I look behind me and see Ginger standing there. "Maybe being assigned here to watch over you wouldn't be so bad." He chuckles as he moves back to his vehicle.

"What the fuck?" I turn on my brother, who actually squirms. "What aren't you telling me, Titan?"

"Drawer has been screwing your cases up for a long time. Mostly to protect those he's in business with but also because your friend Snake..." He pauses, and I'm about at the end of my rope.

"He's not my friend," I spit the words out.

"He also goes by the name Lucifer."

His words stop my heart, and my chest feels like it's spasming. I almost fall over, worried that the man who has tried to kill me numerous times and I've tried to bring down for years is Snake. The man who forced me to marry River. He has her and he wants her.

I see red instantly, and my brother is the man who is going to pay because he's obviously known this for a while. I swing and my fist connects with his jaw. I watch as his eyes roll back, and people are in motion. Even the big guy jumps out of his rig to run to my brother, but I walk away. I don't care if he falls. I don't care if he catches himself. I turn my back on him and reach into my pocket for my wife's keys. I move to her garage and open it up. I head to the gun safe at the back and unlock it. I start pulling firearms. When I feel like I have enough, I turn around to see Scout and a couple Handmaidens there.

"Keys, I need a location on where Snake is," I order her, not caring that I shouldn't. "Riddler, I need your word if I don't come back, you'll take care of River. She'll try to end herself, but don't let her." I pause as the reality of the situation hits me fully. I'm probably heading to my death because Snake will kill me just like I would him. "She's probably pregnant with my baby already." I turn to Thad and give him a slight lift of my chin. "Thad, punch my motherfucking brother again when he comes to." I step out and see that Titan is standing up. He advances on me.

"You can't go by yourself. You don't know where, and you know it's just a trap to kill you." He runs a hand through his long hair. "He'll rape her, kill her while you watch, then kill you."

"I don't fucking care." I get into his face. My heart is seizing in my chest, worried about what she's going through. "I told her I'd protect her. I did this. I brought this into her life."

"No, you didn't. He was after the Handmaidens before. That man…" He pauses and looks like he's trying to find the right words. Everything starts to click into place. "The French guy, LaRue," he says, and Minuet gasps. "He was Snake's half brother. Snake blamed the Handmaidens for his death, but it was Drawer. All three of them along with another guy, who I'm still trying to identify, were in business together."

"I don't fucking care, Atlas." I use his real name. Hermes shakes his head and moves back to his vehicle, leaving with Drawer. "She's my wife. I love her." I turn my back on my brother and stomp to my SUV. "Call me, Keys."

I jump up into my truck and whip my head around when the passenger door is opened. My brother climbs in. I see several of the Handmaidens getting on their bikes.

Titan rolls down his window. "My gear is in there. The password is Olympus. Don't fuck with anything. I'll know. But there should be something on a location by now," he yells at Keys, and she nods.

"Why are you here?" I bark at him as I peel out of the driveway and head to my rental to grab more guns and some other toys I have.

"I kind of like that little purple-haired girl." His words come out soft as if he can't believe he said it. I turn to look at him in shock.

"Are you kidding?"

"Yeah." He tries to chuckle, but it doesn't work. "She was scared, and I thought I could help you. I've never had a sister before, and I need to make sure you're alive to see your kid," he says as he looks out the window.

"Her name is Stormy. She's Thad's little sister." I give him some information. "She's a prospect with the Handmaidens. Goes by the name Poison because she makes a mean drink."

"Well, come on, we have to get going. I have some fun stuff that I brought with me."

River

I come to with my head throbbing. I hear the voice that woke me up, but it doesn't sound right.

"River," Stormy singsongs. "Wakey, wakey. It's time for eggs and bakey." She repeats the little rhyme.

I roll to the side and vomit until I'm dry heaving. When I sit up, my vision blurs for a moment. I look at Stormy and see her pupils are dilated. She's definitely tripping on something.

"Stormy, what did they give you?" I shake her, but she laughs at me and pulls away. She's in panties and a bra, and she's shivering. I'm scared for what's going to happen next. I'm still completely dressed.

"Don't drink the Kool-Aid." She laughs again, and the door swings open. I turn to see two big guys step in, followed by Snake.

"You won't get away with this." I stand up and move in front of Stormy to protect her.

"Out of the way," one of the guards says as he backhands me.

I fall to the side and feel blood running down my chin from my lip being split. I stand up again and get between him and Stormy. My reflexes are off from my head injury. Too many concussions too close together. I know what the doctors warned me about, but I won't let them hurt her. I'm not going to let them just walk out with her.

"Beat her," Snake orders the guards, and they both advance on me.

I hold my ground and start fighting one as the other tries to come up from my side. I swing a kick at him, nailing him. The other guy punches me in the side, and I curl in, my bruised ribs screaming in pain, but I don't stop. I continue to fight until they get the best of me, and I'm knocked to the ground. I cover my face and neck as they kick at me. I roll away, and when I finally look up, they move to the door. I look over to Stormy, who is watching me. A serious look passes across her face before she slides toward me and holds me tight to her.

"I'll die. Don't let me go."

It's the first time since I came to that I actually see Stormy and not the drugs. I push up from the floor and spit the blood from my mouth and then turn back to the door again. I hold my fists up and wave my fingers at the guards in a come-hither gesture. I push Stormy back to protect her. One of the guards advances on me and goes to punch me. I drop and spin a kick, knocking him to the floor. Pain erupts in my upper chest as I hear the gunshot.

Stormy starts screaming, and I land on the mat again. My body slowly shuts down as my brain begs me to get up. My heart clenches when I realize that I'll never get my forever or break the fucking curse of that damn brooch. The other guard moves past me as the other stands over my body. I lie there slowly bleeding out. The guard drags Stormy away by her hair. She screams my name and tells me to tell everyone she loves them. I can't stop it. I can't change what's happening. My eyes flutter and my body shivers. I'm still lying there when the lights are flicked off and I'm left in the dark. I hear Stormy continuing to scream. I hear the grunts as the men rape her, and she begs for death and mercy.

Sobs rack my body. The pain is almost too much, and I lose consciousness.

I wake up. I don't know how long it's been, but I don't hear Stormy anymore. I don't hear anything. The door opens as the light flicks on. One of the guards drags me by my arm toward the doorway, and I fear I'm going to be next. I'm dragged up the stairs, and I notice that it's late in the day. The sun is finally setting, so it must be about one or two in the morning. My shoulder pops and I scream in pain. The guard grunts, turns, and picks me up. He throws me over his shoulder, and all of the jostling has me dry heaving down his back. He curses as he not so gently drops me onto a table. I see blood on the floor, and I worry that Stormy is dead.

"W-Where is she?" I get the words out. My vision is blurry, and I can feel the swelling from the black eyes. My nose burns. I'm sure it's broken. My piercings in my face ache and sting.

"I sent her to a friend," Snake says as he moves toward me. He laughs. "You know your husband had me in his sights so many times but didn't realize who I was." He moves a hand down my arm. "Strip her."

I start to fight again, but my left arm won't work, and because of the blood loss, I'm fading quickly again. I'm naked and lying on the table before I know it. I focus on what is about to happen to me. I can't let it happen. I close my eyes and lock the pain away. I'll die before I let him rape me.

"Give us some time, gentlemen," he orders his guards. "Don't come in unless you hear me say to. You'll hear her screaming. Just ignore it. I'll be tearing her up with my large cock." He laughs as he grips himself. The guards chuckle too and step out of the room.

I look at my left arm and realize it's dislocated. The gunshot wound is in the same shoulder and my upper chest. I slide off the table and hold up my right fist. One time Scout had us practice with a hand tied behind our backs. Right this moment I'm glad she made us do that because this isn't going to be easy.

"You think you can rape me and I won't fight." I raise my brow and shake my head. Then I spit the blood and vomit from my mouth at him, and he dives for me.

"I'm going to teach you a lesson, little girl," he barks as his arm swings out.

I dodge it and realize how incompetent he is at fighting. He's had others fight for him or uses a gun. He doesn't know hand-to-hand combat.

"You're stupid if you think I'm not going to fight to the death. My body belongs to my husband only." I kick out and nail him in the knee. It buckles and he falls. I dance away from him.

"I'll fuck you in every hole, bitch."

He comes at me again, and again I move out of his way. I'm leading him to the corner between the table and wall. I'm going to fuck him up. He comes at me, and I spin around so I end up behind him. I grab his arm with my good one and pull it out from his body as I drop to the ground. I wrap my body around his arm with my feet on his chest. I push with all my leg strength until I hear his shoulder pop. He screams, and I kick him in the face over and over until he's spitting blood out.

When I roll and stand up, he goes to get up slowly.

"Now we match, asshole." I lean my head toward my shoulder that's messed up.

He reaches behind his back with his other arm, and I know he's going for a gun. I slide to the ground, taking out his legs and flipping him around so he's face down. I take the gun from his back and put it to the back of his head.

"Forgive me, Klay," I say as I pull the trigger and blow his head up.

I'll go to prison to end this man. He raped my friend and he tried to rape me. Blood and brain matter splash back at me. I close my eyes. I open them as the door opens, and I fire the gun again. My aim isn't as good, and the guard gets a shot off, but it misses me. I fire again, and the bullet hits him in the leg this time. In the distance, I hear gunshots and an explosion. The building rocks, and I pray that my husband has found me. I move to the table and yank on it until it falls. I hide behind it. When I hear more gunshots and a couple of thuds, I jump up, but there's silence that greets me. Standing there is Klay. He takes one look at me, and I fall to my knees before I collapse in his arms.

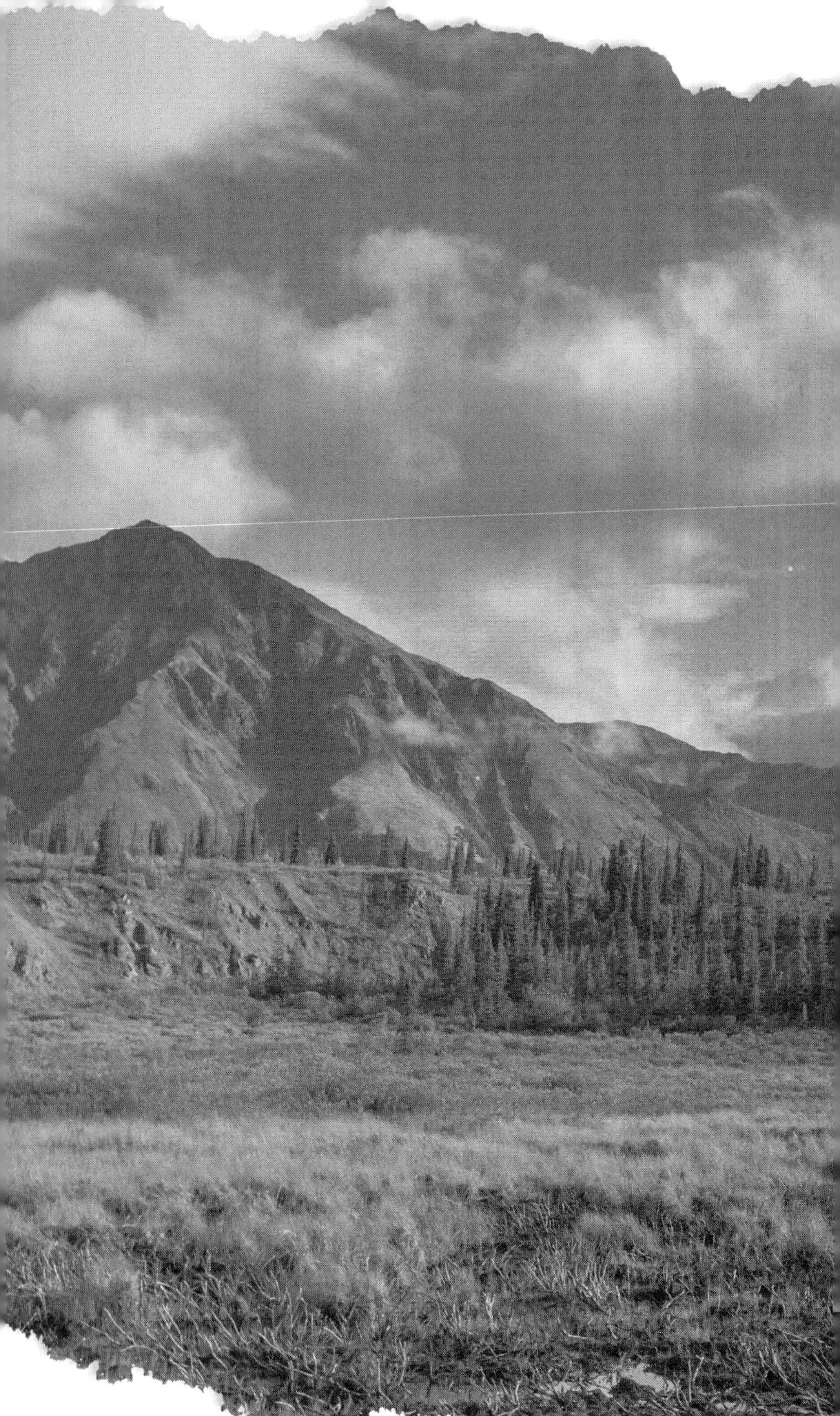

TWELVE
RIVER

I come awake in pain and screaming. All I remember is Snake trying to rape me.

"Shh, baby girl, I'm right here," Klay says next to me. I turn to look at him, but I can't open my eyes to see him.

"My eyes," I cry out and claw at my face.

"It's okay. They are swollen from fighting." I feel his weight on the bed at my hip as he holds me close to him. I cling to him, not wanting to let him go. Every part of my body hurts, even my hair that they pulled on several times when I was fighting them.

"Stormy?" I ask the question against his chest, glad I can't see his face because I don't want to know if he lies to me about her being dead.

"We didn't find her. Titan and Keys traced a vehicle to the airport, where a private jet flew out. They think she was on it. Titan won't stop looking for her."

"Who is Titan?"

"He's my brother."

I remember the man from the fairgrounds. "He tried to help us, but Snake shot him."

"It was only a graze, little sister," a deep voice says from across the room, and I jump. "I won't hurt you." This time the voice is closer, and I can't stop the shiver that races through my body in fear. I want to burrow deeper into Klay's body.

A doctor comes in along with a nurse. I find out I'm at a hospital in Anchorage, where I was medevacked to for trauma care, and that I've been here for three days. I had to have surgery on my shoulder to repair it, as well as fix the damage from the bullet wound. I have several broken ribs, another concussion, and several other injuries. The doctor says I'm lucky to be alive. That one wrong hit and I would have died from a punctured lung from the broken ribs. I'm afraid to ask what they aren't saying, and Klay must sense it.

"You were not pregnant yet, River. It's okay." He squeezes my hand. "We'll rectify that as soon as you're better." His lips brush against my forehead. I fall asleep cradled against his body. Glad I didn't lose our baby. It was something I feared from all the kicks to the abdomen and ribs.

The next time I wake up, Klay is still with me and this time I hear others. I open my eyes and can see Scout standing at the foot of the bed. Thad has her in his arms. I can make out his head as he shakes it.

"I'm okay," I say softly so I don't wake up Klay.

"No, you aren't. When he carried you out of that house, I thought you were dead," Scout cries as she moves to the head of the bed and takes my hand. "Fuck, what did they do to you?" She looks down at me, and I remember seeing her worse than this.

"You looked worse." I squeeze her hand, and she shakes her head.

"This isn't a comparison."

"Any news?" I look at Thad, and he just shakes his head.

"I'm so sorry. I tried to hold them off and not let them take her." I won't tell him that I heard her being raped. I don't know how I'm going to tell him they drugged her up.

"There were drugs found at the house, but Titan said your blood panels came back clean," Thad says, and I hear a catch in his voice.

"I—" I can't figure out what to say.

"You did what you could. We'll find her."

"Okay."

Klay

It's been two weeks since River was taken from me, and we are finally leaving the hospital today. River is in a shoulder brace. She'll be starting physical therapy when we get back home. Titan got the company to pay for a private plane to take us back to Fairbanks. I know he's trying to help Thad find his sister. I'm beginning to wonder if Titan is really into Stormy with how focused he's been on finding her.

When we get back to Ptarmigan Falls, everyone else is waiting to see us. I only allow River to be around them for a bit before I take her back to our small rental. I notice the ground has already been broken on our new place. I'm hoping that it will be enclosed by the time snow flies. We can stay in the rental until it's done. Titan and I went for a style that is similar to a duplex. It has two identical houses attached. They'll share a large four-car garage with a safe room in between them and walls that can slide back to make a large great room. Titan will have a full room with its own cooling system for all his gear and things he'll need.

Every night River wakes up like she does now. Screaming and crying in her sleep. She calls out for Stormy, and I know there is so much more that she's not telling me. She's assured me over and over that they didn't rape her, but I wonder if she witnessed Stormy getting raped.

"Beautiful, talk to me." I hold her with her face buried in my chest.

"It was so awful. They didn't stop, no matter how much I cried out." She pauses, and that's usually all she ever says to me. She won't tell me more. "When they dragged her from the room, one of the guards had a fist full of her hair." Her voice is so soft, almost a whisper. "I remember thinking how dark the purple was against his skin. She fought. Screamed. Begged." Another pause, and this time I hear the soft hiccup as I feel the tears sliding down my chest. "She asked them to shoot her." Panic laces her voice. "They raped her until I fell unconscious. When I woke up, it was so silent. I thought they killed her like she begged them to." She tips her head back and looks up at me. In the semi darkness I see the pain in her beautiful gray-blue eyes. It's like the eye of a storm brewing in them. "Don't tell Thad."

"I won't." I almost choke on the words. "Did they touch you too?"

She shakes her head hard.

"It won't change how I feel about you." I remember seeing her standing there naked and covered in blood and brain matter.

"They didn't. I swear. We have to find her. I know she's still alive." She touches her chest over her heart. "I can feel her right here."

"We will."

I kiss her forehead and try not to tighten my hold on her so I don't hurt her.

"We broke the curse," she says right before she falls asleep. I don't know how she knows, but I feel like it better be broken because we can't handle too much more.

The next morning, I wake up early and take a run along the hills around the property. As I make my way back to the house, I think about settling here. I know that winter can be really cold, but I'll be anywhere my wife wants to be. Right now, that's here.

I open the door and step inside, smelling not only coffee but bacon cooking. I look into the kitchen expecting Titan to be making breakfast but instead I see my wife. Her hair is up in a high, messy bun with wisps falling around her neck and ears. She turns and smiles at me. Her brace cinches her arm to her chest, immobilizing her shoulder in place. I slip off my running shoes and walk over to her. She smells like me. She took a shower, and now I wish I had stayed home to shower with her.

"Mmm, you smell like me."

"I wanted to have you close."

I kiss the side of her neck and then step back. "I'm going to jump in a quick shower. I'll be right back."

"How do you want your eggs?" She smiles up at me. She's in my T-shirt, and I can see she isn't wearing a bra. My brother could walk out of his bedroom and see her like this.

"Over medium. But first you need to put on a bra and some shorts." I reach around her and flick off the burner. She turns, and I lift her up by her ass. She wraps around me. I feel her bare ass and can't stop the grumble as it rolls through my body. I take the stairs two at time until I get up to our loft bedroom.

When I drop her on the bed, I'm tired of waiting to take her. I know she's still recovering, but I need inside her. I need the connection we get when we are that close. I lift her shirt and see her bare breasts. Her piercings closed because she was without her nipple rings. I miss them, but her breasts are still sexy as fuck. I lean down and suck a breast into my mouth, knowing that I can get her off with just nipple stimulation. I take her higher and higher. Her sweet voice moans my name. Her good hand is buried in my hair. I slide two fingers through her folds and feel how wet she is for me. When I slide a finger into her and rub against her G-spot, she throws her head back and screams my name.

With a grip around her hips, I lift her as I drop to the bed and position her to straddle me. I reach between us as she holds herself steady.

She rises up and then slides down my now exposed cock. We both sigh and moan. It's felt like forever.

"I'm never letting you out of my sight again, baby girl."

I moan as I start flexing my hips and bouncing her up and down on me. She has her good hand pressed into my chest, holding herself in place, and her thighs grip my hips. I'm holding her steady with my hands around her hips. We move together, over and over, taking each other higher until my balls draw up. My fingers dig into her hips, and I'm so close. I need her to come again, so I move to her clit and flick it a couple of times. She comes, her pussy flexing around my cock, trying to milk me of everything I have. When I finally erupt, I'm deep inside her. I'm going to knock her up so she can't go far from me.

I settle her on my chest and hold her tightly as we both come down from our high.

"No walking around without a bra and panties as long as my brother lives with us."

"Hey, who started breakfast and stopped," Titan bellows from downstairs.

"We'll be down shortly," I holler back.

"I couldn't get my bra on," River says as she pushes herself up, my cock flexes inside her. "Do you know how long it took me to get my hair up?" She points to the now lopsided bun.

"I'll help you." I can't hide the chuckle.

We proceed to get ready and head back downstairs, where I help her finish making breakfast. When I take my shower later, she's lying down resting and I'm feeling content for the first time in a very long time.

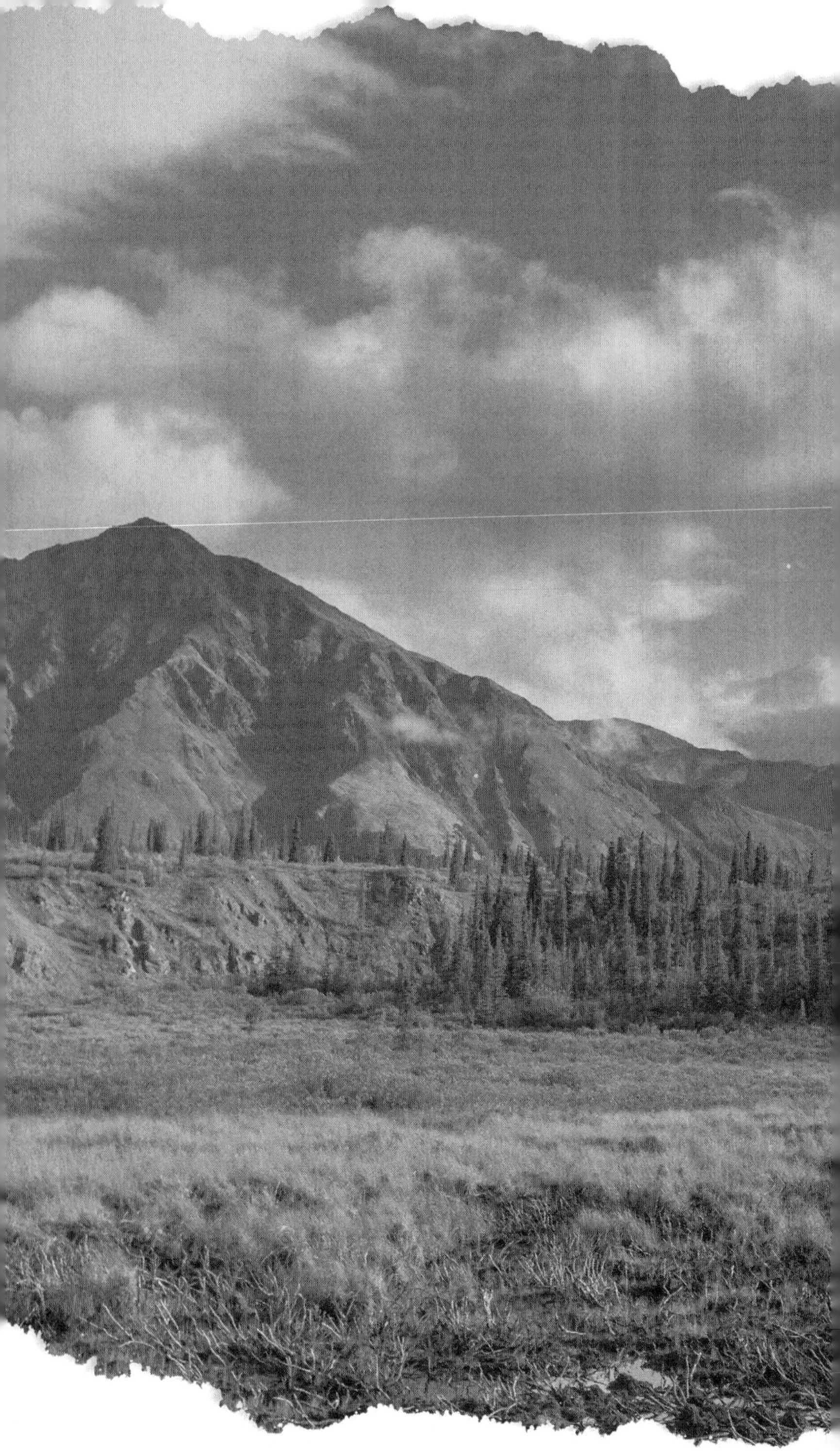

EPILOGUE ONE
RIVER

OVER NINE WEEKS LATER

I stand looking down at the ocean as it beats at the rocks below me.

"Careful, babe," Klay rumbles as he wraps his arms around me.

His palms rest against our child that is nestled in my barely-there belly. I'm almost into my second trimester. He got me pregnant the first time we made love after coming home from the hospital. I'm pretty much all healed up physically. I struggle with nightmares and worry that we'll never see Stormy again. That she killed herself to get away from the man who bought her.

We came to Ireland as our combined honeymoon and babymoon. We renewed our vows in front of all our friends and family, but it still felt wrong without

Stormy there, who was going to be a big part of it. She and Scout are the reason I did it.

Holding the brooch clenched in my fist, I think about the priestess. She threw herself from this cliff because of her loneliness. She only wanted her love. He only wanted her too but thought he had to do what his family wanted.

"It's done." Klay kisses my neck, and I feel the tingles of need and love spreading through my body.

All my parents wanted was for me to find a love like theirs, and I'm sure I have. True to his word, Klay doesn't let me leave his sights. He and Badger are talking about opening a tattoo parlor in Ptarmigan Falls together. Our love of art has brought us closer. But this brooch not only will end a chapter of our lives but open the door to a new future for us. Maybe in the afterlife, the priestess and her love can finally be together. I pull back my arm. My final thought before I launch it over the cliff is that others can find their loves too. I throw it and watch it until I can barely make it out as it falls into the water.

The curse is over.

Now it's our turn to find happiness. I turn in Klay's arms, and he holds me as I let the tears roll down my face. I've held on to that piece for a year. I've let my life be led by that curse, and it's like letting a part of myself go.

Finally, we are free, and so is the priestess.

A cool wind blows through the air, and I smell the ocean. The plants that are still thriving in the

November air waft through it. Taking a deep breath, I follow Klay to the rental car, where we will head back to the little inn we are staying at. Where I know he'll make love to me just like I need.

I don't need anything but him and our child. Klay came into my life, setting both of us off balance, and he rattled every wall I had erected until they crashed down at our feet. I'll love him forever, and I know he will love me too.

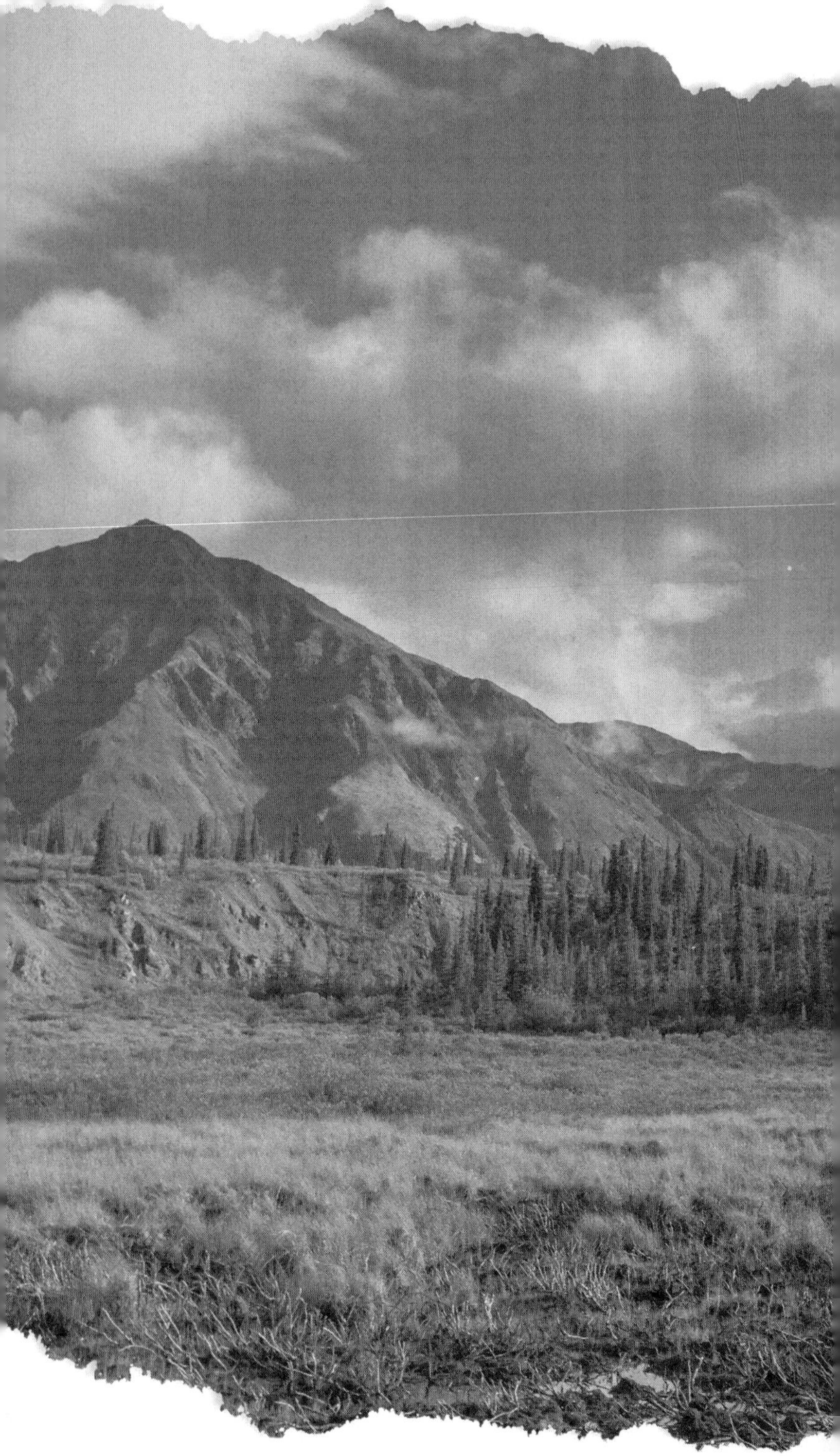

EPILOGUE TWO
KLAY

SIX MONTHS LATER

"Okay, push hard on the next contraction." The doctor looks up from where she is working between my wife's legs. I lean down and kiss her forehead. She's the strongest woman I've ever known. She's the love of my life and keeps me in balance when I feel like I'm not.

"Baby, you got this. Push out our little man." I try for soothing with my voice, but I hear the choke in the words as tears start to come to my eyes.

"Little man? This baby is a beast," River growls and rolls up, pushing hard. I keep my eyes on her, trying not to laugh because she is correct. My son is a big baby. The doctor thought there were twins with how big she got in her second and third trimester, but we'd already had ultrasounds showing it was only one. The doctor tried to reassure River that because myself and Titan are so big, I'd have a son that would be too.

The nurse counts along with the doctor, and I tell her over and over how much she means to me.

"I love you, River. You're my everything."

She cries out a little bit, and then I hear the doctor say something. I look down and there is my son, his head breaching his warm home for the past thirty-four weeks. He's a bit early, but they aren't concerned because of his size and all the tests say he's doing good.

On the next contraction, my wife pushes again, and he fully slips from her body with a loud cry of protest. He's got a bit of a purply tinge to his skin with a fine layer of hair and fluids. And he's letting everyone in the room know he's not happy. Until the doctor lays him on River's chest. He stops and looks up at her before he looks at me. I swear in that moment I'll do everything to protect them both. I reach out and touch his soft head of hair and look up at my wife.

"I love you." I lean in to kiss her, and he lets out a cry. "Listen here, little man, mine first." I kiss her again as she arranges him to let him nurse right away.

A nurse lays a blanket over his body and then steps back, letting us have this moment as a small family.

"Thank you, Klay." River hiccups. "Thank you for saving me and making me live."

"I'll do everything to keep you safe, always." I

brush a hand through her tangled hair and kiss her again.

When the nurse takes our son to the opposite side of the room to clean him up and weigh him, I follow along while another nurse redresses and cleans River up so she's ready for visitors. She insisted she was okay and wants the rest of our family to see him. The waiting room is packed with our families, brothers, and sisters.

Titan and I started a chapter of Drago Defiance here in Alaska, and Scout and River are still running the Devil's Handmaidens even though they were both pregnant. Scout still has three more months to go before she gives birth to her son.

The Alaska State Troopers are no longer actively searching for Stormy, and that caused a lot of hurt with Thad. He ended up walking away from them and now works as a private investigator, searching for her and others trapped in the world of human trafficking. But she is the case that he works the hardest to solve and close. He and my brother work together whenever they can. They'll work with the Handmaidens too, giving them information when the law doesn't help them.

I own a tattoo and piercing parlor with Badger, but I help Thad too. River wants her sister found, and that's our priority.

I look down at my son as they weigh him and do some tests on him. He's perfect, and I'll never take him or his mother for granted ever. I look back to where they have my wife propped up in the bed and are covering her back up. I carry Justice to her and lay him in her arms so he can fully nurse before we let the family all come in.

"I don't know where I would be if you hadn't walked into that bar that night. If not for your love of racing, I never would have found you. I'd still be wandering the world, trying to close a case that wouldn't let me." I feel the first tear roll down my face as I lean over her head and kiss the top with her riot of wavy dark brown hair.

"I think the priestess would have put us together somehow." She chuckles, and I can't hide the smile. "She picked us to break her curse." She's right.

I really appreciate you reading Rattled. Please don't forget to leave a review. To continue reading more from Devil's Handmaidens MC Alaska Chapter, preorder the next book in the series here, Ruined. For a complete list of my books, along with series lists and reading orders on my website.

You might want to consider signing up for Surprises from E.M. for a free story as well as first chance at cover reveals, releases, contests and more.

RUINED
SNEAK PEEK

COMING NOVEMBER 2024

The crowd all stand in front of what is the federal courthouse. I look at it and then back to the podium where reporters are starting to mingle. There aren't a lot of them, but Terry Abbott used to be the former mayor and runs a successful business here in Fairbanks. When he made the call that he wanted to discuss his daughter, reporters came from all over.

I try to stay in the back behind everyone, but Scout asked me to help keep an eye on Skyler and Ryder. I've been with Skyler for years as her nanny and family. Ryder, I met several months ago when his father and Scout got back together after being apart for the last nine years. Ryder is a cutie and well-behaved. I take care of him and Skyler when their parents are working. That's one of the reasons for this press conference today.

It's been six months since Thad's sister, Stormy, went missing. I can't stop the shiver that runs across my skin. I can imagine what she's going through. I've been there. I was raped, beaten, and so much more happened to me before Scout and River saved me, along with the other Devil's Handmaidens in Kentucky. When Scout moved back here to Alaska, I moved with them.

"Minuet," a soft southern voice says my name before I feel her hand brush across my arm. I jump. "It's okay, sweetheart. I'm here." I look up at the woman who sacrificed the most for me. My family said I was dirty and wouldn't take me back, but not her. She rushed to adopt me so I wasn't deported back to Montreal and had no one.

"Hey." I lean my head onto her shoulder.

"I'm proud of you," she says softly. "You came here to help support River and Scout even though you knew it could bring back memories for you."

"I want to help."

I was seventeen when I was kidnapped and then rescued as soon as I turned eighteen. I prospected the Handmaidens because I wanted to help fight this never-ending insaneness of human trafficking. Children, men, and women are all victims of it. But young girls are the most extensively trafficked. I was in the prime age grouping of fifteen to seventeen.

Stormy is older, so in order to keep control of her, they'll have to use drugs and more. She was drugged up the last time River saw her. On the surveillance footage that Titan and Keys found, she was still drugged up and unconscious when they put her on the plane. That plane had only a partial flight manifest, so they never knew where Stormy ended up.

"Hello, ladies and gentlemen. I'm Terrence Abbot. As many of you know, I'm the former borough mayor. My daughter was kidnapped six months ago, and according to the Alaska State Troopers, it's still an ongoing case. But they have no new leads and are putting it on the back burner for now." I watch as Terry pauses. Standing at the podium with him is Scout and Thad. They just got married on New Year's Eve. "My daughter, Stormy, is only twenty-three. When she was last seen, she had deep purple hair." He goes on to give a more thorough description of her. "We just want Stormy returned home safe and sound."

The press conference goes on for a few more moments with the reporters asking questions. Ryder is getting restless. He's five and can only deal with so much.

"Dada, Mama," he hollers and starts to take off.

I grab him back before he makes it to the platform. When I look up, a camera is focused on me. I turn away quickly, causing my blond hair that is loose around my shoulders to fly into my face. I brush it away, and when I look back over my shoulder, the cameraman is still focused on me.

Preorder Now

ABOUT E.M.

E.M. Shue is an Alaskan award-winning romance author. She writes in many different sub-genres but always features badass heroines in gritty situations. As the mother to three grown daughters and two granddaughters she wants readers to be able to see that tough girls can have happy endings too. She is married to the love of her life of over twenty years who she married within months of starting to date, instalove is real.

She published her first book in 2017 after having a dream that later became the Beverley Award winning, Sniper's Kiss. Since her debut, she has gone on to win this award three more times with different books and has published over forty titles.

Join Surprises from E.M. to be kept up to date on all her new releases and appearances.

https://bit.ly/SurprisesfromEM

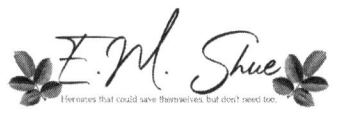

ALSO BY E.M. SHUE

Securities International Series

Sniper's Kiss: Book 1

Angel's Kiss: Book 2

Tougher Embrace: Book 2.5

Love's First Kiss: Book 3

Secret's Kiss: Book 4

Second Chance's Kiss: Book 5

Sniper's Kiss Goodnight: Book 5.5

Identity's Kiss: Book 6

Hope's Kiss: Book 7

Forever's Embrace: Book 7.5

Justice's Kiss: Book 8

Duchess's Kiss: Book 9

Kiss of Submission: Book 9.5

Truth's Kiss: Book 10

Kiss of Secret's Past: Book 10.5 (Coming July 2024)

Knights of Purgatory Syndicate

A Seductive Beauty

A Tortured Temptress

Santa Claus, Indiana Stories

Coal for Kiera: Christmas of Love Collaboration

Hanna's Valentine: A Santa Claus, Indiana Story

Hailey's Rodeo: A Santa Claus, Indiana Story

Love in a Small Town

Caine & Graco Saga

Accidentally Noah

Zeke's Choice

Lost in Linc

Completely Marco

Jackson Revealed

Trusting Jericho

Mafia Made

Her Empire: Mafia Made 2

His Rebel: Mafia Made 5

Her Exile: Mafia Made 8

Tattoos & Sin Series

Doctor Trouble

Vegas Jackpot

Doctor Sinful

Frozen Heart (Coming March 2024)

Stand-alones and Anthologies

Until Tucker: Happily Ever Alpha World

Until Lydia: Happily Ever Alpha World

Rocco's Atonement

Distracting David

Taliah's Warrant Officer

Forever Finn's Kisses

Discovering Tyler

Off Balance

Artfully Bred

Beyond The Temptation: Volume 2 (Blinded by Secrets) (Coming March 2024)

Devil's Handmaidens - Alaska

Wrecked

Rattled

Ruined (Coming November 2024)

Ramsey University Series

Virtuous

Tenacious (Coming April 2024)

Ambitious (Coming May 2024)

Russian Cardroom Series

Ante

Drawing Dead

All In (Coming June 2024)

Prominence Point Rescue Series

Confined Space

Grid Search (Coming September 2024)

Shiver of Chaos

Gambit's Property (Coming August 2024)

Printed in Great Britain
by Amazon